BIVOUAC

A NOVEL
KWAME DAWES

BROOKLYN, NEW YORK, USA
BALLYDEHOB, CO. CORK, IRELAND

Author's Note: A number of short passages in this novel are heavily adapted from the unpublished work of Neville Dawes.

First published in Great Britain in 2010 by Peepal Tree Press Ltd, 17 King's Avenue, Leeds LS6 1QS, England.

Published by Akashic Books
©2010, 2019 Kwame Dawes

ISBN: 978-1-61775-710-5
Library of Congress Control Number: 2018960610

Akashic Books
Brooklyn, New York, USA
Ballydehob, Co. Cork, Ireland
Twitter: @AkashicBooks
Facebook: AkashicBooks
E-mail: info@akashicbooks.com
Website: www.akashicbooks.com

More Critical Praise for Kwame Dawes

for *Bivouac*

"Dawes's novel is a poetic patchwork of waiting, of sliding into the past, casting into the future, but mostly of slow, sensorial limbo in the present . . . Dawes exercises significant stylistic restraint (though it may be Ferron who limits him) so that his flourishes appear like musical interludes, culminating in a final explosion of style and imagination that overwhelms the initial questions the story raises."

—*Maple Tree Literary Supplement*

"*Bivouac* is Kwame Dawes's dark novel about death, politics, family, and sex in a Jamaica that has a 'scarcely understood sense of temporariness and dislocation,' with dialogue that puts you right onto the streets of Kingston."

—*New West Indian Guide*

for *She's Gone*

"A masterly tour de force, the language here is elegant, seductive, and tender, the irony is sharp, the humor subverts, and hope shines through. Kwame Dawes never ceases to amaze."

—Chris Abani, author of *The Secret History of Las Vegas*

"Dawes offers vibrant characters and locales in this diaspora of black culture and strong emotions, bordering the fine line between love and madness between two troubled people."

—*Booklist*

"Set in the American South, New York City, and the Caribbean, this probing novel takes us on a risky expedition to the swampy bottom of the human psyche, a murky world where dreams of love, escape, and artistic freedom swim dangerously close to heartbreak, alienation, and madness . . . *She's Gone* is a work of incandescent genius."

—Colin Channer, author of *Providential*

"*She's Gone* explores the complex dynamics of cross-cultural relationships with deep insight and compassion. The two protagonists, Kofi and Keisha, are gorgeously imagined. In their commitment to searching out the truth, both within themselves and in the world around them, despite their human frailties, Kwame Dawes's lyrical prose explores the true meaning of courage." —Kaylie Jones, author of *The Anger Meridian*

For Lorna,
Sena, Kekeli, and Akua,
Mama the Great,
and the tribe: Gwyneth, Kojo, Adjoa, Kojovi.
Remembering: Neville and Aba.

This is nothing:
tree hill gravel, tactile and tragic,
the pattern of waterscape;
noting these primary tints
I mutter nothing
but the bare sotto voce poem,
like any nude he made
limb or feeling heart.

In this bright or yellow sky
or blue (the symbol is arider than water)
the familiar gesture of the rose
is parched with dry-land laughter but cannot die:
over and under this composed waterscape
delicate crows only are sensuous.
I have this all,
a monotonous bamboo-flute or the immodest jasmine.

"Without Dogma" by Neville Dawes

Unpublished notes of George Ferron Morgan

Already I am beginning to sound like an ungrateful complainer. They say I should be grateful for the scraps thrown before me. So I have a job. I have a job working as a ghost editorial writer for this paper. If the people who have been reading my editorials knew who was writing them, they would be startled, and in some cases quite outraged, I am sure. That Merchant Party lot is still so giddy with victory that the taste of blood is still fresh in their mouths. Peace simply leaves them hungry and thirsty. They would ravage me if they knew. The joke is that the People's Democratic Party lot would do the same. Here I am, suffering because they did not protect me, and yet they would slaughter me for writing editorials for the enemy. Well, screw the lot. None of them have the gumption for revolution. These days, I don't care what they have to say. I feel cheap sometimes. Some mornings I get in early enough to see the two prostitutes who must own this end of Duke Street eating their breakfast out of cheese pans in a shadowy alcove. You can see the fatigue in their eyes—that mute gaze, staring into the asphalt and not seeing. One of them has the most striking cheekbones. But she can't hide her decay. Perhaps I would have judged them once, or simply ignored them, but now I think of myself as a kindred spirit, an old broken-down whore, hustling money from the very people who broke me down. God, I am so cynical. It wouldn't be so bad, this cynicism, if it had the proper effect of making me feel superior, somehow above sentiment and pathos; but what I feel is a truly pathetic gratitude. This is what I have come to. I take my pay with sniveling, bitter gratitude. Who said irony helps?

ONE

The pains came in sharp spasms, cutting through his stomach. He opened his mouth, sucking in air. He tried to force a belch. More air in his stomach. He had eaten too fast, too late.

They had not heard him come in. This was for the best. He did not want to answer questions, to assume the mask of mourning that was wearing thin. It had been a long day, driving from Mandeville with his father's body melting in the backseat of the Volvo. Sorrow was tiring.

He had eaten breakfast at four in the morning before they set out. Kingston was sleeping. They drove downtown, breaking red lights at the deserted intersections. The streets were empty except for the occasional madman or -woman shuffling aimlessly along the sidewalk, smudges against the deep blue of early morning. Ferron noticed a cream Toyota behind them somewhere above Cross Roads. Its lights were off.

"Only dog, madman, an' Christian, to rass," Cuthbert muttered. As if on cue, a cluster of turbanned, white-clad "mothers" strolled in slow, dreamlike motion across Old Hope Road to their morning prayers. The soft sunlight turned their skins to a tender orange, their robes flecked with gold. The wind played with the flowing robes. They vanished behind a thick hibiscus hedge.

Ferron could see the blue tattered flag on a long bamboo pole bobbing above the yard behind the hedge.

They drove along Spanish Town Road where the traffic was a little heavier, and then headed into the country. In Bog Walk, a heavy mist hung in the air. The wiper was on.

They stopped and Ferron stepped behind some bushes to urinate. Farther down the road, just where it curved and disappeared, he saw the Toyota tucked away to the side. He noted the coincidence casually. But from that point on, his body was tense even if he could think of no useful reason to feel that way.

They bought some oranges, mangoes, and bananas from an early vendor. The boy's eyes were full of sleep. He did not have enough change, so they left him with a healthy tip. He was too sleepy even to smile in gratitude.

Cuthbert turned north toward the Mandeville hills.

The early start was important. Cuthbert understood these government departments; after all, he worked in one. Collecting a body involved at least eight carbon-copied signatures and a file full of paperwork. At that time of the morning, with so little traffic on the road, the ride would take them less than three hours. With any luck, they would be back in Kingston before nightfall. The funeral home closed at five thirty, and the proprietor, Mrs. Abrams, wanted people to think she had a home to go to. She would not be there after five o'clock. More critically for Cuthbert, the parlor was somewhere downtown, near Jones Town. He did not want to be caught there after dark. His political connections were not on that side of town.

After the fruit, Ferron ate nothing else for the day.

He looked back a few times to see if the Toyota was still following. He did not see it.

TWO

A crow of a woman with gray patches of hair sticking out of a blue-and-gold silk scarf knotted in front had pushed her way through a crowd of visitors who were gathered around a bed at the other end of the ward, and moved toward Ferron and his mother. They had been standing there by the old man's side for nearly an hour, not speaking. His mother used a cool rag to wipe the expressionless face. She kept whispering to the old man, asking him why he was doing this to her. The old man's bed was the last one before the door to the nurses' office.

The crow was dressed like the others in the group at the far end of the ward: church whites and blacks, which hung on her body at a slant. She held her Bible tight under her thin chest and looked from the bed to the faces of Ferron and his mother. The old man was having difficulty breathing. He looked thin. The woman stared at him knowingly. Two women from the other bed looked over. Soon they were all but ignoring their sick friend and watching this crow-faced woman standing before the old man's bed. Ferron recognized the look. They were expecting a lesson—a sermon.

"'Im soon dead. 'Im soon dead. Yes. 'Im as good as dead, now," she said, turning to them with a knowing gaze, as if expecting applause for her prophecy. "Them always put the worse one dem right side a de door. This one gone, Jesus."

The other women nodded. Ferron felt his mother shaking.

"'Im soon dead. 'Im really look bad." She walked closer to the old man, covering her face with a kerchief. "Soon gone." She sniffed. The other people still nodded, but they kept their distance.

Ferron could hear his mother's breathing quicken. He would have acted, but the woman's audacity surprised him. His mind worked quickly, trying to understand the woman's tone, to decipher something that made sense in it. Sympathy, perhaps, or concern. His mother did not wait.

"Move! Move your sour little body from here, do you understand? I said move! Now!" Ferron's mother shouted into the face of the woman who seemed too startled to move. "If you don't leave this minute I will wrap that scarf around your neck . . ."

"Sweet savior!" The crow-woman clutched her Bible tightly, her face breaking into a twisted network of wrinkles, her mouth hanging open in shock. She sloped her way to the other end of the room, offended, martyred, misunderstood. The others comforted her in low tones, sending admonishing glances toward his mother who kept glaring at them.

"Vultures. Stinking vultures," his mother said, as if trying to help the old man understand. Ferron felt her shame and anger. This was death without dignity. They had no protection from the vultures. The nurse said she could do nothing and suggested that his mother had misunderstood the woman.

"These people mean well. Sometimes them bring a little solace to them what dying in sin," she said with a smile. She was struggling with a syringe package. "When it come to death and damnation, sister, God is no respecter of person." She shrugged her shoulders and walked back to her office. The crow-woman stared across the room with a triumphant smile on her face.

His mother wanted to move the body to Kingston, but there was no money to do so and the doctor said it would be too dangerous. So he would have to stay in this small country hospital, reduced to a simple old man—a peasant, a member of the lumpen proletariat. Ferron felt that the old man would have found it all quite funny; sweetly ironic and fitting. This would have been his end in a classless world, anyway. This was his dream.

He died that night. They got the call from the hospital while they were reading the ninety-first psalm together. His mother breathed what seemed to be a sigh, and then walked into the bedroom and changed into black. She would wear black for three years after the death.

Unpublished notes of George Ferron Morgan

This is Femi's third trip to Jamaica this year and July has not come yet. I think he is coming to cheer me up, but all we end up doing is drinking. Well, he drinks, but I must be a downer for him since I can't find the strength to laugh. Ambassador work suits him just fine. He gets to see his women, and he really loves Jamaica. It is funny, sometimes being with him can really play tricks with you. The jokes, the Shakespearean quotes, the gossip about conspiracies and the memory of that summer we spent traveling across the Soviet Union—he is amazingly good at transporting you until you start to feel younger. But this is Jamaica. We have just come out of a bloody season and everything has changed, utterly changed, and the shadows are thick with desperate people who will kill you for reasons that you will never anticipate. He left yesterday for Rio. I might see him in December, he said. Funny, because when he called to say he was coming, he had me convinced that he was traveling with a contract for me to take up a post at a university in Liberia. He kept asking me if I was ready to go. I said I was. I am. I am ready to go anywhere. He has said nothing of Liberia since he has been here. I am too embarrassed for him to mention it.

Last night we ran into Gregory. He looks quite greasy these days—he sweats a lot, now, which is such a cliché for someone growing fat on power. But I do not begrudge him the extra flesh. At school his lean and hungry look was quite sad; made him hard to trust—and he did suffer a great deal in the seventies. We met at the Sheraton, in the bar. I have not been there in a while, and I really did not want to go for fear that I would run into people like him. But Femi insisted, said I needed distraction.

"My God, George, I thought you was dead, man. You were not on the list?" Gregory shouted this across the room, waving. This is how they talk in Parliament, I suppose. He was red-faced with rum, and, like I said, quite fat. And then there was that big laugh. So I laughed. What I should have said was, "They did kill Appleton on Stony Hill Road. He was on the list too, wasn't he? And we suppressed that well in the paper." But I didn't. I just laughed.

How many people read the paper for news, anyway? "Listening Post" is probably the most popular section of the paper among supporters of the party that forms the government (it was equally popular among them when that party was in opposition). Why? The paper is anti-PDP and the majority of people working here or writing for the paper are, however concealed (at the columnist level) or confused (at the worker level), rabid anti-communists. How anybody of intelligence can take such a stand is beyond me. I similarly cannot follow an anti-Christian attitude. Being against communism or Christianity in terms of debate is quite rational. But to be caught in this inflexible system of animosity is an incredible waste of energy.

THREE

The gas was eating away at his stomach. Acidic. They called it a nervous stomach. That and low blood pressure were his ailments. He was counting the dizzy spells. Today, there had been six. This death was becoming a burden, and yet he took it on, accepted it as his lot, and proceeded to do all that had to be done. Nobody complained. His older brother Lucas was still numb, spending the afternoons reading novels that had belonged to the old man. Nobody knew what would happen when he finished reading. He was sitting with his legs thrown over the side of the armchair reading novel after novel and smoking profusely. He had stopped smoking three years ago when he got saved. The old man smoked. It had been difficult to tell whether Lucas's evangelism was more to win his father to a smoke-free life or to Christ. Whatever, Lucas had poured his zeal into antismoking efforts and, for months, the old man smoked more. Lucas must have given up after a while. Things returned to normal. The old man died a smoker. But smoking did not kill him.

Now, Lucas coughed through cigarette after cigarette, barely burning each stick. Most of the family seemed to understand that everybody had their private ritual of mourning. Only Clarice, their sister, ventured to remind him that cigarettes were expensive these days.

She was protecting her money; Lucas had taken to borrowing a lot of late.

A small delegation from the church had visited the house the Sunday before to offer their condolences. They were hot in their heavy clothes and carried their Bibles and hymn books. They seemed, though, more intent on trying to speak some sense into Lucas, who had missed three important services since the death, than on condoling with the family. Lucas barely acknowledged their presence when Ferron opened the door for them. They stood in a huddle, silhouetted by the large window that filled the den with the orange glow of dusk, whispering to Lucas, who sat back, almost parodying the old man, listening to their admonitions. Finally, Lucas stood up and turned to the window. The delegation was silent.

"He is my father. I rejected him. I turned my soul from him, and now he is gone." Lucas's voice was calm and evenly modulated. "We look alike, me and him. You can see that. Look at that. Look at that." He lifted the bust of the old man and put it beside his face. "We could be brothers, right? And it was badly done, everybody says so, but you can see the resemblance. They made him look older, ten, maybe twenty years older. This is what he was going to look like. Maybe it was intentional, a prophecy, something to keep him growing with us, you know?" He paused, placing the bust back on the side table. "So why can't I smoke too? Don't I deserve to feel what he felt, sitting here? This is his seat. Don't I deserve it, to feel . . . him?"

"Brother," one of the sisters tried to sound patient, "this is not of the Lord . . ."

"Aahhh! Not of the Lord," Lucas said, turning to her.

Ferron was startled at how much his tone was like the old man's. "Not of J. Christ Esquire, eh?" He laughed.

Somebody breathed, "Lord!"

"That is what the old man would say," Lucas continued. "I have never read his books. Do you understand what that means? Do you? I never read any. None. Zero. I read everything else but . . . No . . . I am doing what I have to do. These are his shoes. These are his . . ." He paused. Ferron was expecting him to break down, and stood, preparing to clear the house of the delegation. But Lucas did not start to cry. He was trying to find the right words. "This is . . . this is him," he finished, leaning back in the chair.

The delegation could not get him to say any more. He was busy reading. They gathered around him and prayed. Ferron looked over to the telephone room and noticed Clarice sitting there in the half light, chewing at her nails and watching everything. Her face was expressionless. The delegation finished their prayer and promised to come by again soon. Lucas did not look up. They left as quietly as they had come.

Ferron watched Lucas lean forward and peer through the window to watch them leaving. He turned away quickly as Lucas looked over to him. He heard Lucas chuckle slightly. There was silence for a few minutes. Lucas lit a cigarette and continued reading. He turned a page. By now it was too dark to make out his facial expressions. He was a shadow.

"They think I have gone mad now," he said slowly. Ferron could hear his smile. "So how the hell I must explain to them what I am doing when I don't even know myself, eh?" He laughed softly. "You just do what you have to do." That was one of the old man's stock lines. Ferron caught it, so did Clarice, sitting in the telephone room. They started to laugh. Lucas laughed with them.

Then they grew silent, at first trying to find something to say, but gradually accepting that there was nothing to say, that the darkness was a shelter. They sat in the dark for a very long time.

Unpublished notes of George Ferron Morgan

I have been taking taxis to work every day. I need a car. I think I will get a white Toyota Corolla. That is what all the political thugs are driving. They must be quite reliable. It is a long way from the Rover three-liter. But we are a long way from those days. I am spending a small fortune on taxis. The strange thing is that I don't feel the urge to drive myself anymore. I want to be looked after. I used to love driving. That summer we drove across Europe to Moscow and then across Russia, that feeling of command of the road, that adventure, it seemed like second nature. But we are a long way from all of that now. A white Toyota Corolla.

The difficulty here is that I have never worked in a firm or company before. It has nothing to do with whether one is making money for the company. That is fun. It has to do with the structure and relations in the office. I find it incredible that this office is set up as a large room, with some sixty or seventy chairs and about forty desks. The first problem is noise. The perpetual clicking of typewriters (I have to type at great pace, writing nonsense, to avoid going mad) and the jabbering of people on the telephone or the interviewing of and by working-class voices inhibits any kind of creative work. What we have is noise as in a garment factory and the quality of the output is similar.

FOUR

When Ferron came home the night after the Mandeville journey, Lucas was slumped in the corner, his head thrown back, with a book in his lap. He snored with a slow untidy asthmatic wheeze and grunt. A cigarette smoked in the remnants of his supper which was catching flies on the floor. It was hot and Lucas was sweating. They did look alike, Lucas and the old man: the nose, the thick glossy beard, the high forehead. Lucas, however, lacked the haughtiness—the old man's condescending confidence. Even in his sleep, Lucas looked humble, almost defeated.

In the kitchen Ferron found his way around with the help of the refrigerator light. He was afraid to turn on the fluorescent bulb which hummed loudly and startled roaches into scurrying and flying around the room. The noise would bring someone out. He did not want that.

He ate the cold curried chicken and a few clumps of rice, quickly. He could see the line of light under the door of his mother's room. He considered going in to tell her he was back, but decided against it. The stillness of the house was why he had lingered in Half Way Tree for more than three hours after Cuthbert had dropped him off. He had missed the last bus and was forced to take a taxi home.

He took a glass of water to his room. His stomach

had already begun to churn by the time he had taken off his shirt and trousers and thrown himself on the bed. He tried not to think about it there on his back, staring at the slanted lines of light from the street on the wall. Music from the bar across the way drifted into the room. The pattern of dog's alarms relayed from fenced-in yard to fenced-in yard. He listened instinctively for the sound of barking to fall into a lull, then he relaxed.

The old man would be on his back on the stained sheet in that funeral home where they had left him as if fast asleep. Or perhaps he was in heaven trying to understand what to do with so many years of paradise. Maybe he was waiting for the ancestors to construct that long bridge of light with strips of material from the moon, peeled off like onion skins, a path for him to walk from soil to soil, to the Port Harcourt black earth where the pebbles would be familiar again, and the sound of feet, stepping above, comforting in their rhythm. If not there, he would have to be in hell. No fires, just the waiting, a sad desperate waiting, surrounded by illiterates. Like the rest of them, Ferron needed a narrative for his father's afterlife.

Family story had it that the old man had confessed Christ a month before his death. Ferron had noticed him listening to late-night sermons on the radio, and once, three weeks before, the old man had spoken during a family prayer hour. To call it a prayer would not have been an accurate description of what he said. He simply spoke. His eyes were open and he was smiling:

"We need some peace in this house too."

This was his addition to a list started by Clarice and extended by Mother. Lucas, who was muttering in tongues and flavoring each insightful utterance with a heartfelt "amen," went completely silent after the old man had spoken. It was Ferron's turn, and he quickly thanked God for everything and ended the prayer time.

The old man was beaming. Nobody spoke. It was hard to tell whether his look was of irony and self-mockery, and an awareness that he was messing with the minds and hearts of his family, or whether he was sincerely seeking peace with his maker. The problem was that the look was a well-cultivated one. Clarice had been certain that it was mockery, because she walked off muttering how it was no wonder the Lord never took any of them seriously. But Ferron thought he saw something else, something like peace in the old man's eyes. They never spoke again about that moment until after his death; then it became evidence of his salvation. They were grasping. Everybody knew this.

So, it was possible that the old man was resting in the bosom of Abraham, somewhere in Zion. The old man would find it all quite funny.

Although he was expecting it, the first wave of pain in Ferron's stomach caught him dozing. He got up quickly and ran to the bathroom, grabbing an old *Star* from the dresser.

It was impossible to read it—the pain was so intense. He leaned forward, wrapping his arms around his stomach. With his head between his knees, he could smell the stench from his uneasy stomach. The smell made him more nauseous. He shivered, rocking his body, talking to himself, praying: "Oh God . . . no Lord . . . Can't take it . . . Can't . . ." He felt light-headed, weak, yet he was acutely aware of everything around him. The silver of the taps, the red in the shower curtains, the pink of the toilet mats were all vivid, clearer than normal. He was able to focus on details like the pattern of black spots in the tiles at his feet. He was waiting for the break—the sudden calming of the body after the pains. You accepted its coming with faith.

There was a lull in the pain. He tried to focus again, wiping sweat from his forehead. Then he felt his stomach heave upward. He ran to the tub and retched. Everything came spewing out. His stomach continued to contract as if trying to force the emptiness out of him. The effort weakened him and he sat on the floor, leaning against the tub, trying to slow his breathing to calm down, to stop the hiccups. He cried. He cried sitting on the floor; a full-throated crying. He cried as he washed away the vomit from the bathtub. He cried as he stumbled slowly to his room.

He opened the lower windows in the bedroom and tried to stop the crying. It was useless. He lay back on the bed, now naked, and felt the tears run into his ears. He felt nothing, just this longing to stop trembling, to stop the pounding in his head.

He drifted in and out of sleep, his stomach was still uneasy. He dreamed of warm places, white mint milk caressing the pain in his stomach. At four o'clock, he heard Lucas coughing in the bathroom. After that, Ferron slept.

Unpublished notes of George Ferron Morgan

There is a man who has worked here for about forty years, a Jamaican brown who obviously thinks he is white. He is incredibly opinionated. He evidently thinks the paper has deteriorated since the time of de Lisser and he is fighting a stubborn battle to get it back to that style. He considers himself the authority on good English and his manners are atrocious. After working here for forty years he was, up to the time I joined the staff, only a senior reporter. His resentment was very deep. Recently the editor promoted him to the post of assistant editor and he is very pleased because he can now say that he is running the paper. I pity the editor. Scattered through the office are browns holding on to their past status, contemptuous of the young blacks who pack the office, earn large salaries, converse in very harsh patois, and are essentially noncreative. A few of them have been given encouragement by the editor. He has little to choose from. One girl got a First Class Honors at UWI in English and it seems to have killed her manners. At any rate she is not at all attractive. Another (I do not know his background) writes a column occasionally. He cannot write. But he maintains the kind of arrogance which he thinks a columnist should have. He is pathetic. He types at great speed, churning out badly written stuff.

FIVE

Ferron was standing on the sloping concrete ramp waiting for them to wheel out the body on the metal tray that was stained with the blood of somebody else. The old man had bled, but it was all internal.

The morgue squatted on a hill. It was a square, flat-roofed, single-story building set off from the hospital like a glorified outhouse. One expected to see the words *DANGER: HIGH VOLTAGE. KEEP OUT* painted in red on the walls. The slopes leading to the white building were lush Mandeville-green, and neatly kept. The narrow concrete path, just wide enough to hold a hospital trolley, was lined by a blooming hibiscus hedge. A woman in black stood to the side of the building, staring at the grass at her feet.

She seemed to be waiting for something. She held an olive-green rag over her face. Ferron, tired of waiting and deprived of Cuthbert's somewhat distracting humor—he had gone into town to try and do some business—became fascinated by this woman. She did not seem to notice him, as if she thought that the rag over her face made her invisible. Ferron wondered if there was something wrong with her teeth.

She removed the rag from her face, spat, then assumed the same posture. It was a familiar gesture. Spitting like that was something people did when they were near something foul-smelling. They did not have to smell it or see it; they just needed to know that it was there. Soon she added a few more ritual gestures: the short but audible exhaling of air through the nostrils, the waving away of nonexistent flies, and the grunt of distaste.

Ferron was surprised at his annoyance with her. He wanted to ask her to wait somewhere else if she was so damned uncomfortable. He turned impatiently to the doorway of the morgue. A policeman in uniform strolled out, wiping his face with a handkerchief. He walked by Ferron and spat into the lawn outside the building. He was followed by a short, barrel-bellied dark man, another policeman, who kept wiping his hands on his trousers.

"Sunday, eh. Sunday. Kill a man 'pon a Sunday. Is like them do it to spite we, man." He was talking to the fellow in full khaki who brought up the rear. Ferron recognized him as the morgue orderly he had spoken to earlier. "Shit, man. Is like dem jus' say, officer, Monday is a workday, Blodoi!" He formed a gun with his fingers and jerked the arm back. "See work here."

The woman walked tentatively toward the two officers.

"Close casket, man," the uniformed officer said.

"Nobody can fix dat face," the other policeman laughed. "Unoo mus' fix dat air conditioner, man. In dere stink."

"Officer . . ." The woman suddenly looked very old.

"Oh, lady," the plainclothes officer turned to her as if he had remembered something.

"When I can tek him, sar?" she asked.

"You can tek him anytime," the officer said. "You sure 'bout the statement, now, right?"

"Yes sah," she nodded.

"Is yuh son?" he asked.

"Yes sah."

"An' is t'ief shoot him?"

"Yes sah. Goat t'ief. Dem come in an' shot 'im, sah . . ." She took a deep breath to continue.

"An' yuh sure yuh neva see dem?" the policeman interrupted before she could continue what was obviously going to be a lament.

"No sah. Neva see nobody, sah." Her head was bowed. It was clear she was lying. It was as if she wanted them to know this.

"Tek 'im, then," the officer said, sighing. She nodded, avoiding their eyes, and started down the path to the hospital complex.

Ferron could see a broken-down Morris Oxford parked on a grassy embankment beside a cream-colored Toyota Corolla. Two men sat in the backseat of the Toyota. Another two men sat on the hood of the Morris Oxford staring up the hill. They wore long black rubber boots and tattered hats. Farmers. She walked toward them.

"You gwine look at the nex' one?" the khaki-clad orderly asked.

"No sah. Later. Enough fe this morning, boss." The officer was already making his way to the walkway. His uniformed companion was staring down at the group by the Morris Oxford. The car had started and was moving toward the main gate.

"What the rass!" He scratched his head. "Them gone."

"Oh shit," the khaki-clad man said, looking at Ferron.

"Funny business, eh? Ah tell you, man, is one of dem man deh do it. I know it. She have 'bout eight son. Dem always a fight. See down there? Is a murderer down there." He was pointing to the Morris Oxford.

"Look, I gone," the senior officer said as he strolled off.

The orderly winked at Ferron, who was about to blow up. He had been waiting all morning and now they seemed intent on letting him wait for the entire afternoon as well. The orderly followed the two policemen down the path. "Wait deh, officer, jus' look on one more nuh. This man come from morning, an' . . ."

The two officers stopped and turned in a smooth, almost rehearsed fashion. They looked at Ferron as if they were noticing him for the first time.

"Which one this?" the officer asked, still looking at Ferron. Ferron stared back.

"The man weh drop over by Whitehall." The orderly was moving back to the morgue door. "Simple thing. The doctor look on him already, them say 'nothing strange.' Yuh jus' have fe sign. Look an' sign."

"Your old man?" the officer asked, moving back up the path. Ferron nodded. "Hell of a thing. Hell of a thing. Rum is a terrible thing." The three disappeared into the morgue. A few minutes passed. Ferron watched the Morris Oxford crawl along the main road and disappear around some buildings. He wondered whether they had abandoned the dead man.

The officers walked out, the taller, uniformed one first. He spat into the grass and continued down the path digging into his pocket for keys. The shorter officer followed, nodding at Ferron as he passed. Ferron could hear the squeak of wheels as the orderly pushed a trolley out. The smell of blood filled Ferron's nostrils. It was not a smell of decay, it was cleaner: fresh blood.

"Ready?" the orderly asked. Ferron noticed for the first time that his clothes had bloodstains. Human blood, Ferron thought. The short man was businesslike. His forehead shone with sweat as he worked with quick jerky movements around the trolley. He kept reaching to swat away something from his overlarge ears. He looked up at Ferron with old, bored eyes. The irises were light brown. "Ready?"

The body was tightly wrapped. The old man seemed smaller, thinner than Ferron remembered. He wondered what his father was wearing underneath those sheets. It was hard to tell if he had on anything at all. He did not ask. He wanted to ask if they would let him take the sheet, but he hesitated. He thought of the newspaper in the back of the Volvo station wagon. They would need it if Cuthbert's car was not to reek of the dead. The body did not appear to be frozen. The old man would smell.

"Yes . . . Alright, business time now . . . let me see now . . ." The orderly flipped through some sheets sloppily clipped onto a piece of plyboard. "Morgan, nuh?"

"Yes," Ferron said.

"Well, yuh better check him out . . ." The orderly looked up at Ferron and smiled smugly. Ferron felt as if he was being dared. "You have to make sure is de right one." It was like a commercial transaction. "Father, nuh?" he asked casually, still studying Ferron's reaction.

Ferron assumed a nonchalant air. "Yeah." He looked at his watch. The orderly searched for a pencil, found it in his breast pocket, and began to write.

"Name?"

"Morgan, Ferron Morgan . . ." Ferron stopped. "Whose name?"

"Yours . . ." The orderly smiled.

"Well, they are the same." Ferron tried to laugh.

The orderly had not heard. "Name," he said, peering at the sheet in front of him.

"Morgan, Ferron Morgan . . ."

"Spell it . . ."

"F-E-R-R-O-N," Ferron said slowly.

The orderly wrote, pausing after each letter or two to admire his work. Then his brows tightened. "Then nuh the same name this?" He compared the two words. "Cho, man, me say your name. *Your* name, boss, *your* name." The orderly was erasing furiously.

"That is my name, Ferron Morgan. We have the same name." Ferron was becoming uncomfortable. He was worried about the sun beating on the body in the trolley between them. He was aware of the absurdity of the dialogue. There was something dreamlike about the whole affair. "I just said—"

"You mean you and the man name . . ." he frowned at the clipboard, first sounding out the syllables, then saying them, "Ferron Morgan?"

"Yes, sometimes fathers do that." His sarcasm was lost on the man, who was now smiling. "What?"

"Shit," the orderly laughed. "Then somebody might read this an' believe say the dead man nuh tek out him owna self."

It did not matter that Ferron was not laughing. The orderly chuckled at his own little joke for the remainder of the time the two were together. Later, Ferron would tell the joke to Cuthbert, pleased with himself.

Ferron studied the short man carefully, trying to construct a fiction around his wrinkled face and bored eyes. The orderly scratched his head with the pencil. Sparse clumps of hair littered the glowing surface. He would make an ugly corpse. Ferron wondered if the orderly ever imagined himself on the trolley. That kind of thinking must come with a job like that. The orderly slipped the pencil behind his ear, which glowed transparent against the sunlight creeping over a huge Bombay mango tree behind the morgue. A line of sweat trickled along a vein that snaked down the middle of his forehead.

"Well, is him this?" He lifted the edge of the sheet at the old man's head. The nose was stuffed with blood-stained cotton. The cheeks were bloated. The old man's face was discolored—bluish. Ferron could see a hint of cotton sticking out of the corner of the mouth, mingling with his graying moustache. His eyes were closed. It was not like sleep—there was nothing there. Nothing.

"Who you taking him to?" The orderly fanned a fly from the open wound on the right side of the head. "Travis?"

"No. Abrams," Ferron said. He wanted to ask about the wound. It was a tidy incision just above the right ear.

"Abrams? From where? Not from Mandeville?"

"No, town. We taking him to town." Ferron tried to discern any reaction from the orderly. There was none. He nodded and then leaned forward, peering at the wound.

"It will alright," the orderly said, pointing to the wound with his chin. At first Ferron thought he was talking about the heat in the car and the body. "Tha's which part the doctor cut, eh? You cut it right there soh, an' then you strip it back—jus' fe see the brain, yuh understan'? After dat, yuh jus' pull it back over. No need to sew 'im up, really. Mos' time yuh can jus' hide it. No-badda fret 'bout it. Is a simple job, you know. Dem can jus' stitch up clean-clean and pack the head good-good. No problem at all. Nobody will notice," he assured Ferron with a smile.

"Right." Ferron could feel the acid starting to churn in his stomach.

"Well, the res' looking quite good, eh? Not bad. Could be worse." He waited for Ferron to agree.

Ferron nodded.

The orderly craned his neck to look under the right ear, then satisfied with his appraisal, he turned to Ferron and reassured him: "Easy job. Them can fix him up no problem. Even me could do it."

Ferron smiled stupidly.

"I know some Morgans, you know? Your people from Mandeville here?" The orderly was organizing the papers on the pad. Ferron just wanted to take the body and leave. He looked down into the parking area for Cuthbert. The Volvo was parked on the banking. The Toyota was gone. Cuthbert was not around.

"From Mandeville?" the orderly repeated.

"No, St. Ann."

"Oh . . . St. Ann. Nooo . . ." He pulled the sheet over the old man's face. "I know the face though."

"Television," Ferron mumbled. A part of him hoped his father would be recognized. The squalor of this piece of business had cheapened the man's death, deprived him of dignity. It embarrassed him.

"No . . . no." The orderly passed the clipboard to Ferron, indicating where he should sign.

Ferron looked back down the hill. Cuthbert was standing beside the Volvo eating from a box of Kentucky chicken. Ferron waved him to come up.

The orderly took the clipboard from Ferron and walked back into the morgue. A few seconds later he was outside. "Nuh this man use' to run the Hilo supermarket hereso in Mandeville?"

"No," Ferron said. "Not him."

"Jesus Christ, the man favor Missa Morgan! Mus' be a jacket business," he laughed.

Ferron watched Cuthbert amble up the pathway with a bundle of white sheets. In the parking area, the Morris Oxford was back. This time the woman walked with three other women. They were dressed in white and their heads were tightly turbanned. The driver of the car, a skinny dark man wearing a red tam, did not get out. The women were singing as they climbed the hill to the morgue.

"Shit, I know them woulda wan' come with this foolishness," the orderly said, hurrying inside.

Unpublished notes of George Ferron Morgan

A supposed poet gave me some poems to read. They are awful. He is not a poet. Again the pathos. I shall suggest that he send them to publishers. The pathos is that he thinks he is a poet. Again the arrogance, the lack of humility. The lack of a sense of scale. I do not have the spare energy to deal with this.

Financial success is unbeatable in a capitalist country and we have it, running into many millions. Just keep up the form, invent new gimmicks, and advertising will do the rest. It cannot ever be important that there are not enough readers to increase sales because readers read to nonreaders and that nonreader is our man and his ignorance must not be disturbed. Keep it that way for as long as possible. The Adult Literacy Program was and is a failure and now we are going to kill it, but delicately, not as crudely as the Jamaica Information Service. What else do we need to kill?

I must try to probe the backgrounds and working careers of the black people in here. Could it have been a straight political choosing? There was obviously no "cultural" choice; speech will tell you—and speech will suggest that Tivoli Gardens is very strong. Again, my ignorance of offices might be responsible for this. But it is appalling what an effort has to be made by them to speak English. Further resentment comes from the articles I did on the "Great West Indian Writers" in my clearly idiotic effort to let them know that we have had quite gifted writers—world-class writers and there is something of a tradition of good writing. But this fell on deaf ears. And here in the office, it annoyed the younger writers. Too much space given to these old writers, they murmured. Perhaps they are right. After all, these are new times, and that lot were all brainwashed by colonialism and it is roots time, reggae time, man time now. Ah, my Revolution has finally arrived! Revolutions are for the young. I am now, at best, an old campaigner. Well, what to do? My point has been made and as I am clearly not going to be paid separately for doing those articles, I don't care if the others are not published. I hope the two I did will at least lead to some sales for those writers.

SIX

They drove back without stopping. Few words passed between them. Cuthbert drove slowly. He was not sure how he would explain the body to the police if they were stopped. Ferron had somehow not gotten a receipt or whatever was needed from the orderly. Ferron kept looking into the back of the car. A year ago, he had dreamed of his father's death. They were riding in a taxi, a black cab. His father sat beside him staring out of the window. He was dead.

"He will alright," Cuthbert said.

"I know. It's just strange. It feel strange," Ferron said. He looked back again. This is when he noticed the Toyota—the cream-colored one with the two men. The car was behind a truck, but Ferron recognized it from the headlights. They were on in the broad daylight. He kept looking back. The Toyota stayed with them.

After about an hour he asked Cuthbert to stop at a roadside kiosk. Cuthbert nodded and stopped in front of one of the vendors. Ferron did not move. He looked through the rearview mirror, watching for the Toyota. The Toyota slowed and parked at another kiosk a few yards behind. Ferron stepped out and walked to the vendor, still watching the Toyota. The men were not buying anything. Four boys were shoving plastic bags full of oranges into the windows of the car.

"Buy me a bag too, eh?" Cuthbert said.

Ferron bought two bags of oranges and came back to the car. Cuthbert started the engine.

"Wait," Ferron said. He was staring in front.

Cuthbert looked over at his cousin. Ferron peered into the rearview mirror. Cuthbert turned around and then looked in front.

"You feel they following, eh?"

"What you think?" Ferron asked.

"Maybe. But is a free country, man." Cuthbert started the car and swung onto the road. The Toyota followed.

In Kingston, Cuthbert lost them. He drove into Beverly Hills at breakneck speed, took a secluded side road, and then doubled back down onto Hope Road. By the time they were in Cross Roads, there was no sign of the Toyota. Cuthbert smiled. "Bitch!" he said. They continued downtown to the funeral home. It was still light when they reached.

SEVEN

For the next two days Ferron had the old sensation of wanting to run. This time he was trying to resist the urge, but in the past he'd done that kind of thing a lot. When things became too pressured, he would pack a bag, take a van downtown, and get on the first bus to any destination that suited the length of time he had to escape. If he had a day, he would take a bus to Edgewater—that dry landfill of a suburban experiment which overlooked the Kingston Harbour. He would walk along the scarred, salt-white roads toward the large marl hill where only the most rugged of bramble survived. It was always hot, blazing, unrelenting. He would crawl down a narrow pathway to a small crevice in the face of the hill. This faced the sea and was completely hidden from the road. He would sit there and stare at the sea for hours, simply allowing his mind to empty. Nothing happened around there. The occasional plane would land at Palisadoes, a boat would trundle by, and a few sea gulls would dive at some prey on the water. Nobody would know where he was. He would disappear for the whole day relishing his return to the dorm to the chorus of "Where you was? People was looking for you . . ."

When he needed to disappear for longer periods, he would take the bus to St. Mary. It was always to the same place, a small community called Clonmel where an old girlfriend of his had grown up. He had spent one summer there working with a church theater group and had become a part of her family. They always welcomed him with fried fish, buttered hardo bread, and milk. They asked no questions. Mr. Robertson was a plump, cheerful man who worked for the Education Ministry, but farmed in St. Mary. His wife was a retired school-teacher who still ran the small primary school built on their property. All their daughters, seven of them, were either in boarding school, at the university, working in Kingston, or abroad. The parents lived alone and welcomed Ferron's visits. He would stay for several days, and they would let him stay aloof, go for long walks, or simply talk about anything at all. Nobody knew where he was. Nobody needed to know.

There was one farther destination he would use when he did not want to see anyone at all. He'd used it when his need to write had been greatest—or his need to make sense of his life. There was something about this place—like a place of punishment. Whenever he felt he'd hurt someone, or failed himself, he'd go there to wallow in self-pity, to suffer from the fear of being alone in the woods, with fantasies of being attacked or killed by some wandering person. The plyboard shack was in an open lot somewhere in Jack's Hill. He'd discovered it when he was going on a long hike into the hills. Some-one must have intended to live there, but changed their mind. They had probably thought better of such seclu-sion. It was stark, had scarcely any furniture but was quite dry. He'd made a mental note to return there when he needed to. One evening, on a whim, he decided to take the chance. It had been after an argument with Lucas, or something painful like that; he found the hut and spent the night. The fear nearly destroyed him, but he left the next morning feeling somewhat cleansed by the ordeal. He spent three more nights there during the very difficult period of examinations and final assignments; then it became a writing retreat. Nobody, as far as he could tell, knew about the hut, nobody except one of his hallmates. He thought he needed to let at least one person know, so that if he died there, the body would not be left to rot to nothing.

The last time he'd been there was when the wedding to Delores was in its first incarnation. Two weeks before the event, he'd panicked. He was also working on several postgraduate assignments. At home he grew silent. He could feel heaviness and gloom consuming him. It was not long before he knew he was going to go into the hills to wait out the wedding. He watched friends and relatives planning everything. The old man asked him what was wrong. He did not answer. The old man said laughingly, "You're going to bolt, aren't you?" Ferron laughed, and the two just sat there laughing, and nothing else was said.

He'd bolted the next night. It was that escape to the Jack's Hill hideaway that now most occupied his thoughts . . .

When his sister and Delores eventually found the hut and tried to bring him home, he'd been there for several days. There were clothes strewn all over the bed and sweat-stained socks stank in a pile behind the door. Books and letters were scattered where he had left them after a frantic search for a lost chapter of his thesis. This document supposedly contained the secret to the completion of the project he was working on. He'd found it, but was wrong. The writing was weak and the only relevant aspect of the paper was a sentence that was in itself a naive misinterpretation. He stopped working on the assignment. He'd brought several packs of beer with him and stayed indoors drinking. After the beer he went hungry; he had no more money.

He'd spent hours standing at the window looking out into the woodlot. The earth was parched. Whatever grass survived the onslaught of the tractor tires was withered. Huge tire marks crisscrossed through the dried mud. The trees started uncertainly a few chains away from the building. There were stumps and felled trunks tangled among the hardy bramble. Gradually the forest assumed a sturdier character. Beyond that was darkness.

He'd seen the sky purple gently above the treeline, heard the faint sound of traffic on the highway about a mile away. It would get dark soon. Acid burned in his stomach. He'd felt hungry and worried, certain he had an ulcer, but the pink antacid fluid had dried up in the bottle that lay on its side on the floor. He couldn't afford another bottle. Probably couldn't even make it out to the highway . . .

The food was finished but that hadn't worried him. Hunger would draw something out of him. It produced a mediocre poem about writing. The creative secretions stopped.

He went to bed early and did not sleep until it got light. No clear moment of structured thought came to him during the night. In the afternoon, when he could think clearly, he could not recall his thoughts of the night before. He burned the poem and placed another sheet of paper in the machine.

His eyes began to ache again. He rubbed them and winced at the pain. They felt heavy and watery. A grating irritation, like a tiny grain of gravel under the eyelid, cut into one eyeball. He held the eye open until it dripped tears. He hoped that would wash out the particle. When he let the lid fall, the pain was still there. He dragged the lamp with its naked bulb into the bathroom. He stared into the mirror, the light blazing under his chin. The image was grotesque. There were sunken holes on his eye sockets, his cheeks, and under his lip. He pulled open the damaged eye again, raised the lamp to the side, and winced as the glare pierced into his cornea. It was bloodshot, but there was no foreign particle in the eye. He blinked and blinked again. The eye still hurt. He put down the lamp and doused both eyes with water. His nose was flowing. The irritation got worse. He thought of rubbing the eye until the pain became so unbearable the eye would grow numb. He resisted the urge.

He must have fallen asleep because he did not hear the car drive up, nor for a time hear the two women whispering outside the door. He heard the knocking and the calling. He didn't move. Nobody was supposed to know where he was. They continued to call. The knocking stopped. There was a long period of silence. Perhaps they feared that he was ignoring them in anger. Then it must have struck them that perhaps he was dying inside the room, so the knocking became more insistent. He did not move. He wanted them to go away.

He could hear them walking around the house. Clarice did most of the talking. She kept calling his name and then she started to shout. She was silent for a few seconds, then she sent Delores to check the back for a door. Delores said she could find no entry. Perhaps he wasn't there and Harry was wrong. Was there another cottage nearby? Delores thought it better that they left. Clarice wouldn't leave. She said he could be dying inside and in need of help. Delores didn't say anything. Clarice began to knock on the door again. She kept calling his name.

He stayed still. His eyes were open now. He thought about what he must look like. His shorts were filthy but he had already worn the red ones so much that it became painful to put them on. He had grown used to the smell of his body. He made sure to keep a clean shirt and trousers in his bag for his return trip to town. He'd have to hitchhike home so it was important that he at least looked decent. His hair and beard hadn't been combed for days. The knots were tight and hard. He didn't want them to see him like that.

Clarice had started to push against the door. He thought of getting up to open it, but his body did not respond. He just lay there smiling and wondering whether she would manage to break it down. Clarice was a determined woman. Delores's attempts at discouraging her were futile. Delores said that perhaps somebody else lived there and it could be very dangerous if they came home and found two women trying to break in. Clarice told her to either shut up and help or just go and sit in the car. Delores shut up and helped.

The door was rotten so after a few blows it cracked and Clarice got her hand through to unlock it. The room was filled with glaring white light. They had parked the car directly in front of the door and the headlights were on. He turned his head and squinted into the glare. Clarice stood with her legs slightly apart, silhouetted by the light. She was wearing a light skirt and her legs were outlined through the fabric. She whispered his name with caution. He kept staring. His eyes dripped. Delores leaned against the door looking away from the bed. He watched her. Clarice walked into the room and moved toward the bed. When she was very close, he moved. She stopped and called his name again.

He sat up on the bed and propped his chin in his hands, his elbows pressed into his thighs.

"You alright? You alright?" Clarice peered into his face. "Your eyes are red." He closed his eyes. "This place is a mess, man. Where is the window? Delores, don't just stand there, open the windows, eh?" Delores moved quickly to the window in the bathroom. She did not look at him. She stayed in the bathroom.

"I can't believe you wouldn' tell anybody where you were. What is wrong with you? Mama is very worried about you." Clarice was moving around the room trying to create some semblance of order. After a while she gave up. "Hey? Hey? Talk to me. Are you alright?"

He stared into a corner of the room. He wanted them to leave. He began to smell the room properly now. The waft of air from the open window and the cracked door stirred up the latent musk. He chuckled to himself.

Clarice said: "Delores wants to talk to you. Now hear, she didn't want to come so don't get upset and start bawling her down, but I think this is pure foolishness so you better talk to her. I mean, you must be gone mad, man. She deserve better. It's alright if you want to vex and confuse everybody else, but this woman hasn't done anything to be made a fool of like that . . ."

"Clarice, please . . ." Delores said from the bathroom.

"You see? She is afraid of you. Anyway, right is right. Please. Explain yourself, sir." Clarice stood in front of him. He stared at her feet. "My God. You haven't even combed your hair!" She placed her hand on his head and raised it so he had to stare at her face. She had on makeup: pink lipstick—he hated that; she must have come straight from work. "You look bad, sah. Delores, come out of there. Come. Talk to him."

He got up and stretched. Clarice stepped back. He got down on his knees and reached under the bed for his sneakers. He sat on the bed and slapped them on the floorboards. Then he pulled them on. He ignored the laces.

"You can't just change your mind about a wedding, okay? There are other people involved, not to mention Delores. You can't be so selfish, man. People will start calling you a madman."

He got up and moved to the bathroom. Delores moved away from him as if he was a madman. She sensed something disquieting about his silence. She *was* afraid. He turned on the tap and splashed his face.

"Look, you better say something. The cake is still there, the food is spoiled, but we can work that out. De-lores's parents will sue if this thing doesn't happen . . ."

"They won't . . ." Delores's voice trembled.

He turned to her and felt a deep pity. He could only see a shadow for her face but he could feel her fear and despair. She looked so small and vulnerable.

"They will," Clarice said with emphasis. "Now,

you better get your act together . . ." She stopped as he walked past her toward the door.

He turned around and looked at them, smiled slightly, shook his head, and then continued. Stuffing his hands deep into the pockets of his shorts, he trotted down the stairs. He stooped for a few seconds to regain his balance, then his shadow cut through the light and vanished into the dark.

"Come, Delores. He wants to go home now," Clarice said. But when they did not hear the car door open they looked out and saw him walking toward the edge of the woodlot. Clarice shouted his name. He did not turn around. He continued walking steadily until the forest swallowed him.

He felt the wetness of the thicker grass in the bush. He could hear the two women talking to each other. He watched as Clarice ran to the car and started it up. Delores stayed at the door. Clarice maneuvered the car toward the spot where he'd disappeared. He stood behind a tree as the lights glowed through the bushes. She moved slowly, the car rocking on the tractor-tire marks. When the lights were off him, he moved farther away, though still at the edge of the bushes. She blew the horn and shouted his name. She did this for about ten minutes and then she stopped the car. The air of the lot was cut through by the din of crickets and frogs. After another five minutes, Clarice moved the car back to the shack. Delores stepped down to the ground and walked toward the car. Clarice stepped out and they stood beside each other staring directly at him in the forest. They remained in silence for another few minutes until it became clear that nothing would happen.

"Let's go," Delores said. "Let's go."

The car bumped through the woodlot toward the dirt road that led out to the brightly lit highway. He stepped out of the bushes and stood staring at the car. One of them must have seen him, because the car stopped. He stayed still. He saw Clarice's shadow emerge from the car. Slowly, Delores's shape emerged as well. He did not move.

"I thought you said you saw him. You see him?" Clarice asked.

"It was nothing. Just a shadow," Delores said, moving back to the car. "He's gone."

He watched the taillights bump along the lot until they turned onto the paved road, and then all light was gone. He stood in the darkness listening to his heart pulsing. There was something complete about this whole thing. He knew that it would not be long before he walked out of this place, went back into the world. Delores understood what it all meant. In a peculiar way, he was sure she'd been expecting it to happen. He walked slowly back to the hut, his head bent down . . .

Back in town, to life, no one spoke to him—not really. The jilting of Delores was like a death best left ignored. He did not see her for almost a week, and then they met for lunch, and soon they were an item again. This time marriage was not mentioned. He had tried to explain to her what had happened several weeks later.

"I needed to escape, to get away . . . It was all coming down." He spoke slowly.

"You needed space . . ." she said sarcastically.

It had been the gradual movement back into the

mundane of a relationship without direction that assured Ferron that there was no future with Delores. They would get married, have children, but he was sure they would be divorced. The apparent reason would be his unfaithfulness, but the real reason would be sheer disinterest. He had known this for sure.

But then the rape had injected something emotional into the relationship. At least she expressed real anger. That she blamed him was clear. That she felt it was unfair to blame him was clear. But that she still, despite that, blamed him and felt great anger toward him was even clearer. It was hard for him to ask her what she'd wanted him to do, whether she'd wanted him to fight, get shot, even die for her, whether that is what she expected. It was hard for him to tell her that he, too, had been so scared, so petrified by everything, that the night had left with nightmares. He could not tell her that because in many ways, he did blame himself. His sense of relief at being alive after it was all over was something that filled him with guilt and left him incapable of even fighting with her. But the worst truth was something she never actually said, but that they both knew to be true. Before the rape, all affection had dried up between them. Now, after the rape, the absence of affection had to be filled with some other emotion because they were connected by this trauma. What he felt was resentment, even anger, at the idea of having to feel something, having to think of themselves as two people who needed to support each other. He felt her withdrawing from him, and he did not mind her doing that. He disliked himself for feeling incapable of giving her the affection and care she needed. He felt overwhelmed by deep anxiety about being near her, about being in this mess with her. Everything about that night was a massive weight, a very inconvenient mess. He recognized that what she had experienced was far worse than anything he could have felt, but managed to push that farther back in his mind. The more she grew cold with him, the more she seemed to blame him for what had happened, the more he felt himself pulling away emotionally. After a few weeks they started counseling with Dr. Davis, a bearded ex-Catholic priest who seemed to have no clear agenda for their sessions. It became clear that they were covering their anger and resentment with something that looked like boredom and disinterest. After a testy session which revealed that they were no longer being physical with each other, Dr. Davis had suggested that perhaps they needed to remind themselves why they were together in the first place. If the bed was a "site" of contention, and if, "as was understandable," it brought back unpleasant feelings that had to do with the rape, then they should start meeting in public places. So, for a month or more they'd been meeting in public places, trying to "regain some balance." The meetings were flat and dull unless they quarreled. Even then their fights were not loud, but filled with snide remarks, sarcasm, heavy silences, and very short sentences. The meetings continued largely because neither was willing to be the one to admit that their relationship had been purely physical. His father's death had provided a good excuse for avoiding the last two meetings, and now, with the visit to the clinic, he was going to add another excuse. He was not going to tell her he would not be able to make it. He would just not show up, would call her later and tell her why.

Now, even though he knew that if he bolted again everyone—*everyone*, including his sister and his mother—would see him as a predictably weak person, a selfish person, the worst thing that could have come into Delores's life, he still wanted to run. He needed to run. And he might have taken off to the shack had he not known that they would come to find him there and, more importantly, had he not felt so sick in the stomach. To go up there with the plans for the funeral still not put together and his sickness at such an intense level would have been too much even for him. The pain in his stomach had gotten progressively worse. He could feel the churn of acids by midday. The best he could manage was escape into Kingston proper. He would avoid places where he might run into friends and family. He would head downtown to the Institute's library or to one of the downtown high schools to watch a football match or something. Each day he would plan something. Now, with the sickness, his plan was to go to the clinic on Maxfield Avenue, a rough area on the edge of downtown where his mother had taken him as a child, but where he did not have to go since he could have seen doctors at the university. But down on Maxfield Avenue, he would be away from everybody for at least half the day.

Unpublished notes of George Ferron Morgan

I have really learned nothing in three months. The greater joke is that I am supposed to have learned something about the newspaper business. It is impossible not to feel despondent when someone says to you—a big fifty-five-year-old man—"Oh, you will get the hang of it." Especially when the person is an illiterate. There are techniques but no mysteries. Putting a paper together editorially is a matter of intelligence. Getting at the news requires minimum intelligence, a lot of time, and an ability to bully and threaten. You also need to have a sense of your own importance and to press it firmly. This I cannot take on at my age. Strictly speaking, I am not interested in the news; it makes me reflect too much on the inevitability and finality of death. I am sad about having wasted so much time "working" and not writing enough. All I had wanted to do was to finish three books in 1982. Now I must aim at 1983, which means publication in 1984.

I always had doubts about the amount of work I'd put in at the Centre. I had to do it—we had to eat—which seems so melodramatic, but it was true. After the two years that I put the family through, everyone needed some fat days. So I worked. And from 1973 to 1976 I worked eighteen hours a day from Monday to Friday and six hours on Saturday and sometimes on Sunday. I also drank a lot. I stopped drinking for six months in 1974, and again after September 1979 (though, at the time of the Centre crisis, I drank heavily one night at Femi's house with Andrew present—all rather embarrassing now). Now, I don't drink. It is hard to know why. But I do know, if I started to drink again, what it would make me. It is enough to be unemployed, but how miserable it would be to be constantly drunk, drinking what money we don't have—and drinking with whom? I suppose I never was one to drink unless there was a performance to make it worthwhile—a stage, an audience. Now, no one would drink with me. They would just feel sorry for me. They have fled like rats. It is as if this thing is a disease.

They shouldn't mind. Here we are in the glorious decade—Restoration Jamaica. Now we can put off puritanical austerity and buy American apples and grapes, import good shoes from foreign, and to hell with turning a hand to make fashion. The whole thing seems like such a pathetic farce now, an absurdity. When I listen to the music, Bob Marley is dead, and it is as if everyone is smoking cocaine or that crack to make music—it is so manic. I am too old to even understand what a party is. The clowns are back in their suits and it is now fine to cheer on a light-skinned beauty queen. Everyone is getting fat. Even the good Trotskyites are buying and selling real estate. Why would anyone want to see me now? I am dead, really. Dead.

There is no mystery about their decision to sack me from the Centre. They had to defend this newspaper, but just who demanded it, I cannot guess. He had to get Burns to be the hatchet man (of course, Burns lied to me about his pleading for one year more), but they are all in my debt and they will pay. They know they owe me a great deal. And here is the pathetic irony of it all, that no one could have planned better. I am sacked for challenging the integrity of this newspaper. And who hires me to write editorials when I have nothing left, but the same newspaper? If I had the energy, I would despair at the pantomime of politics. Now, the editor is trying, as an Oxford man, to make it up to me. Imagine that—his loyalty to me as an Oxford man far exceeds his loyalty to me as a human being unfairly done in. But they don't know how much they have destroyed me. Every single one of that lot. What they have done to my family. They have succeeded in creating some of the conditions leading to Ferron's setback. Yes, the irony of my being here is sharp.

EIGHT

First there was the long squeal of brakes and tires. He waited. It was like stubbing a toe, he thought—a short span of time, a few seconds, and then the pain reaches. There it was. Crunching metal, a thud, then the sound of glass. Ferron imagined a rain of splinters across the street.

"'Im dead! 'Im dead!"

"Jesus Christ!"

The rest was just noise. People were running to the scene.

Ferron stared through the blackness of his palms past the pink line of light seeping in through the tiny space between his little fingers. He framed her in the slit and moved with her like a camera. She was a flash of white light, a quick blur darting out of frame as she rose with unexpected speed for a pregnant woman to go outside to join the others.

He did not move from his seat in the clinic's waiting room. His heart thumped. Somebody could have been dead out there. Bleeding. He closed the tiny peephole and listened to the shuffle of feet, the doors opening and closing, the exclamations, the questions, the clamor of horns and engines whenever the door opened.

"Next . . . Mitzie Lowe?" A man's voice. Ferron looked

up. It was a teenager with a card in his hand. He had just walked in. He looked around. Ferron was the only one in the waiting room apart from the nurse who was still on the phone.

"Mitzie Lowe," the boy said in a louder voice.

The nurse looked up. "You might as well go in, you hear," she said to Ferron. The boy discarded the piece of paper and walked out of the office. Ferron went in.

The doctor was an Indian with a smile. He spoke like a television commercial with an Eastern lilt: "Eat, avoid stress, no milk—lactose is acidic, you know—rest, and exercise." He was scribbling down a prescription. "Tell your mother sorry; tell her to come see me, eh? Walk with crackers. Cream crackers. No salt. Forget the prescription, man. The nurse will give you some antacid. Tell her is for your mother. They are friends. No coffee, no cigarette, no booze. Feel better now. Good. Try that. Always try eating right . . . The next person is Mitzie Lowe, you remember that? Easy: Mitzie . . . Just say Mitzie, alright? Or Lowe. Either one. Pregnant woman . . ."

The doctor did not wait for answers; he just kept on talking. Ferron walked out, tired. The lobby was full again. Evidently the crash victim was either dead or was in perfect health. Otherwise he would have been in the clinic already. Mitzie, the pregnant woman in white, was back at her seat, fanning herself with an old *Gleaner*. She seemed more excited now, as if she wanted to talk to somebody. The rest of the lobby was completely still. People stared into space. Patient. Ferron looked directly at her.

"Mitzie Lowe?" He smiled.

"About time too." She got up with exaggerated strain.

She walked toward him. She was smiling warmly.

He moved to the side. She followed him. He shifted again and she moved with him.

"But what is this?" She stopped. Mitzie had a streak of amber running along the side of her hair. She fiddled with a necklace. "You don't wan' me to pass, sir?"

Ferron moved aside. She walked by him, brushing her hips against his hands. There was more than enough space to avoid contact. He decided to wait for her to come back out.

Ferron bought a corn bread and butter from the Rasta vendor whose cart was parked in the corner of the parking area. Ferron ate slowly, watching the doorway for the pregnant woman.

She walked out, rummaging in her bag for something. He looked around. There were no cars in the parking area. She did not look like a car owner. Then she looked up and around, spotted the vendor's cart, and moved toward it. Ferron walked out of the shadow beside the cart. She smiled. He smiled back. The Rasta was hustling.

"Yes, dawta, yes. Juice, baby mother?"

"Ice water, in a cup," she said. She was looking at Ferron. "What?" In the sunlight, her eyes seemed crammed with riddles. They sloped slightly, the eyelashes thick and long.

"What?" Ferron was suddenly uncomfortable. She was too confident, able at any time to embarrass him.

"You watching me like that . . . What happen?" She was taking the ice from the Rastaman.

"The bredda like what 'im see." The Rastaman grinned. Ferron was grateful for the support.

"Oh. Is that so?" She turned to Ferron.

"Maybe."

"Maybe, nuh." She laughed, chewing the crushed ice.

"You sure yuh nuh wan' nutting sweet in dere, dawta? Lickle coloring?" The Rastaman had not made a sale and he did not seem about to charge Mitzie for the ice.

"No," Mitzie said, still looking at Ferron.

"Too sweet already, eh?" The Rastaman laughed. "You too perfect already, eh, dawta?"

"Exactly." Mitzie moved away from the cart and used her eyes to indicate that she wanted Ferron to follow.

"You got through?" he asked.

"Yes, man." She was chewing on the ice and staring into the street. Ferron followed her eyes. Between the cars you could make out splinters of white, red, and yellow glass. "You woulda believe seh somebody dead, eh? The way the people dem was a gwaan. Old neaga too bad."

So nobody had died. Ferron was about to ask her what had happened, but hesitated. This was not what he wanted to talk about.

"When are you due? If . . ." He was not sure what her reaction would be. "I mean the baby . . ."

"Next week," she said, grinning at him.

"Next week! You shouldn' be in hospital or something?" He tried to make it sound funny.

"Yuh never hear say black woman strong. Cho, we jus' drop de pickney dem one place, wipe off, and is gone we gone 'bout we business." She did not take her eyes off his as she spoke. "A soh we hard."

"I see." Ferron knew she was laughing at him. He did not mind.

"Man!" It was an insult, an expletive. She looked

back at the street, crushing the ice and sucking in the cold water at the bottom of the cup. "Me notice how you never even look up. You just siddown dereso, like you never even care."

"You mean the accident? I was tired." Ferron saw that she was not convinced. "I just don' like see dem tings, you know. Is like people just waiting to see a dead man. What do they say first: ''Im dead! 'Im dead!'?"

"Tha's not the only reason . . ." She stopped eating the ice.

"No?"

"No."

"So why you run out there, then?" He knew he was pushing it.

"It coulda be my bredda out there," she answered. She was looking away from him now. "Or my baby father. A girl must know them things early-early so she can plan the party." She was laughing again.

"You know you bad."

"Well, is the truth." She threw the cup on the side of the street.

"Littering," he said instinctively.

"I don' like when people try tell me wha' fe do, you hear." There was an edge in her voice. "So which part you walking?"

"Half Way Tree," he answered. He did not want it to be over already. "Wha' 'bout you?"

"Jus' around soh." She nodded up Maxfield Avenue. "So what 'appen to the car? Garage?"

"No car," he said.

"No car, big-big uptown man like you?" She laughed. "Barbican, right?"

"What?"

"Is Barbican yuh live, right. Or is Norbrook?"

They lived in Barbican. He did not think it was so obvious. "You feel you can just read people like that, eh?"

"Most times. Most times I can tell what a man thinking. Like you now, you married, right, or engage, but you look on me and you start ask yourself what you doing. But you cyaan control yuh feelings, brother." She smiled. "Then suppose I wasn' pregnant, eh? Suppose you see me slim up and ready, man, you woulda jus' lef' the girl long time; is lie? You woulda jus' rush me, eh? Right thereso in front a John Public."

"Sounds tempting." Ferron liked her boldness. He did not have to do anything, just be.

She laughed. "Come, walk with me. Is jus' down so. It safe."

He followed her.

"So what she name?" she asked as they walked.

"Who?"

"Your wife?"

"No wife. My ex-fiancée is Delores." This was the first time he had described her in those terms.

"So it wasn' me?" She pretended disappointment.

"No," he said.

"Somebody else?" She did not seem bothered about prying like this.

"Me," he said.

"Oh." She looked at him quickly, and then continued to walk slightly ahead of him. She asked no more questions.

I prefer to call it a low-grade depression, but even the word depression seems trite when I think of what happened to my brother. He wanted to die. So he drank. If you asked him, he would say he did not want to die. But he knew he wanted to die. I don't want to die. I just don't mind dying now. I feel dead. Man feeds on usefulness. I have never felt as useless to the world as I do now. I used to think that I would relish that kind of useless—that I would take the time and write books, travel, reconnect with friends. But that is the kind of thing that people happy with the world and with their minds do— people with friends who are not treacherous, people with money. I have no money, I have no prospects. I add nothing. So dying would not be terrible—it does not frighten me. And this is not bravado.

Felix, the taxi driver who picks me up in the morning, said he was sure he saw one of those white Toyotas loitering around the house when he came in at five in the morning. I asked Felix why he had come at five. He said he comes early so he can sleep a little. He can't sleep at home. Too many people—his nieces and nephews, his grandchildren, and so many people he and his woman have taken in. So he sleeps in the car outside the gate, waiting for me. He said he saw one of those white Toyotas with four men. He thought a politician was in the house meeting me and that they were waiting for him. I told him there was no politician in my house. He stopped talking. He seemed very sad. He shook his head. Then he told me that five nights before he had dreamed of a baby. He did not explain. He just went on to another story. He said he was in Trelawny two days ago digging yams from his ground in his home district. It was around dusk. He heard the hoot of a patoo. He said his skin got all prickly. He stopped and said nothing else. Then when we were near the parking lot, he asked me if I had heard about the former member of Parliament who was gunned down in Jack's Hill last night. I told him I had heard. He said, and I can't forget it, "All now, you would t'ink all this murdering woulda done, but now is the time to clean up shop."

When I came out of the car, he said I should mind my step. I decided to be tragic and give him something to quote if I was gunned down that day. "No man knows his time or hour. Fear is a waste of time, Felix. You know that."

He did not say a word, he just smiled in the way that people do when they are talking to a complete buffoon.

NINE

"What the hell you mean you never took the report?" Lucas was shouting down at Ferron, who tried to ignore him, watching the television. Mother was tense. She had tried to calm Lucas, but he wouldn't listen. Clarice wrote in her notebook. They had just finished their Sunday dinner. They missed the old man. Nobody sat at his place. Clarice had unintentionally prepared a setting for him. When she was clearing it, Mother told her to leave it, so they ate with his empty plate staring at them. Little was said. Ferron went through a few of the details for the funeral. Clarice and Mother asked questions. Lucas stayed silent, concentrating on his food. Clarice asked what Lucas would be doing. Ferron said he had not thought of that. Clarice and Mother both turned to Lucas, who stared in his plate. Ferron became uncomfortable. He could tell that they had been talking in his absence, and it had something to do with Lucas being the oldest and the funeral plans. He stopped talking about the plans he had made. But after dinner it exploded.

Lucas walked back and forth around Ferron, interrogating.

"I never said I didn't take one; the man never gave me one." Ferron tried to stay calm. He didn't want to fight. "He said it was routine. Hemorrhaging from the fall. That was it. I saw the coroner's comment."

"Didn't give you one?" Lucas moved to the window. "You mean you hear them giving him autopsy, you see police and everything, and you don' ask nothing? That's what you telling me?"

"Bingo."

"Don't fucking *bingo* me! Don't take that tone with me, man!"

"Lucas!" Clarice shouted, trying to drown Lucas. "You don't have to talk like that . . ."

"Jesus," Mother said. She was patting her chest.

"What the hell wrong with this man, eh? You can tell me? Just tell me that and I will be quiet." Lucas directed his words at Clarice. Then he turned to Ferron. "Is like you feel you have special right to know everything, eh? You think you know every damn thing, right?"

"That is your field, man." Ferron stared at the television. It was an old movie. He had no idea what he was watching.

"Your father! Your father fall down a set a stairs, fall down in a stranger yard, and dead. Your father. You don' ask who de people was, you don' ask no question. You don' care what the police say, you just carryin' on like nothing happen. Your father." Lucas hovered above Ferron. "Well, let me tell you something. I asked a few questions, you know. I did. Who you think those people was, eh?"

"Oh Christ, you gwine start this again." Ferron stood up.

"No, listen to him," Clarice said.

Ferron sat. "So you into this foolishness too?" He looked at his mother. She looked down. She too believed.

"Foolishness, nuh. Who the hell find the place for him, Mister Ferron, eh? Who?"

"You tell me," Ferron said. He was sure what was coming.

"Just tell him what you know, man," Clarice said. Her lips trembled slightly, her fingers toyed with the loose threads at the end of the sofa.

"Vera Chen. Senator Vera Chen, alright? That man there . . . that Walters guy, not the old man . . ." Lucas looked to their mother for support.

"The son," she started, looking at Ferron. "The man with the bike. It's the old man's son. He doesn't live there." The man with the bike had come to the house when they were talking with the old man. The man said he was his son. The young guy went to the back and came back around with a few planks of wood on his head. He gave his condolences, climbed onto his S90 bike, and balanced his way out of the yard.

"Yes. That one. One of her boys them," he continued. "What happen, you shut up now, eh? You never know that, right? What about that, now? And you know what time the old man fall down the stairs? You know what time? Eight o'clock, right? Tha's what the man said, right?" He waited for Ferron.

Ferron stared at the television. He did not want to hear any of this. The man was dead; that was the end. He found these theories all too tempting. He had toyed with them and found them attractive for they gave him anger, provided him with an enemy, somebody to blame. It was a useful outlet, not unlike what he felt about the men who had raped Delores. But this was a fiction, a strained construction, and he knew it. He stopped thinking about it.

"Answer me, man!" Lucas shouted.

"Yes."

"The man said he didn't know . . ." Their mother was trying to calm Lucas.

"No he didn't," Lucas said. "He didn't."

"Well, he didn't know." Clarice was becoming impatient again. She kept looking out to the front gate.

"Too high up with *all* his responsibility to know, too high up." Lucas said "all" with an elaborate outstretching of the arms.

"He's been through a lot," Mother said.

"Stop talking about me as if I not here . . ."

"Like him is the only one who been through things!" Lucas shouted. "Hey, hey, this busy-busy business not going to bring your woman back, you know? Go talk to her, beg her, do something, but don't bring you problems into this place, man. I sick of it. It's your father's death now, alright? All of us have suffered loss, now. Not just you."

"Do me a favor, eh. Just do me a small favor and keep your blasted mout' outa my business. You understand?" Ferron was now standing and pointing at Lucas.

"Don't point at me!" Lucas's eyes flamed. He flung Ferron's outstretched arm from his face, and then stood to his full length, throwing out his chest. "Don't do that!"

"What is wrong with both of you, man?" Clarice shouted. "Ferron, sit down, sit down, alright?"

"So why the hell you never went for the body yourself, eh? If you so damned jealous, if you think maybe it was your responsibility, why you never get off your fat ass and go for the body? I never beg to go, alright?" Ferron was shouting.

"Ferron." Clarice's eyes said, *I understand.* She dared not let Lucas notice.

Ferron waited. Nobody spoke. Ferron sat down.

"One o'clock in the morning. One o'clock! That is what the hospital people say. One o'clock when them bring him in. And them tell the nurse that him was drunk. Drunk." Lucas sat down at the other end of the room. "That piece of crap, lickle work. All for that. The old man was getting senile. Chen of all people. You couldn't warn him?" He said this to Mother.

"He needed a job," Mother said softly.

"That piece a crap?" Lucas waved her off.

"It was something. He needed something," Mother said. "We needed the money."

"Well, him really get something," Lucas muttered. "What you watching?" He had turned to the television, as if nothing had just transpired.

"So what are we going to do?" Clarice asked. Nobody spoke. "The police could investigate. Maybe somebody did push him."

"The boy wasn't there that night. The father said so," Mother said to Clarice. There was resignation in her voice. Ferron understood. "I saw the stairs. There were two identical doors. He picked the wrong one. There was no bannister, no railing. He fell."

"You believe him, nuh?" Lucas said.

"He is my husband, Lucas." Her voice was breaking.

"You believe that man, right?" Lucas said again.

"Man!" Ferron glared at his brother.

"What is there to not believe?" Mother asked. "Why would anybody want to kill him, then? He was where he was supposed to be . . . Where they wanted him . . ."

"You pushed him too hard; he never wanted the work." It was barely audible, but everybody heard. Lucas stared into the ground. Nobody said anything.

Mother sat still for a few seconds and then spoke. It was as if her voice was coming from far away, another space: "We got condolences from Senator Chen this morning. A nice card. We also got one from the prime minister and the leader of the opposition. Aunt Louise won't be coming. She has no money. We got a notice from the owners of the house. I am going to stay with Gene, until I can get some money together for a new place. You will need a job, Lucas, and somewhere to live. You should get over this and get some help from your church friends. Clarice, you will have to move into the house in Ensom. Ferron, Cuthbert says you should stay with them in Stony Hill, till you get organized. My new place won't have too much, so we can divide the furniture. Your father owed some money on the car. I will take care of it. We have about a month and a half to two months to leave this place, so you children need to start planning. The owners would want us out sooner, but they decided to show some mercy.

"Tomorrow, your father's friend from Nigeria will come. He faxed the details this morning. He will stay in your room, Ferron. And Lucas, if you want to trace the path to your father's death, maybe by finding somebody else to kill him, please go ahead, but do it quickly because the cremation is on Friday. I am going up to Newcastle to pray. I need somebody to drive."

Ferron knew she was completing business for her last family meeting. There was something final about this ritual of splitting up the family. She was making it formal, official. Mother carried out her final task as parent. She stood up with effort. Her eyes were soft, heavy with this small request. She wanted somebody to have heard her.

They called her "Mother Miraculous" for her impossible ability to transform tragedy, catastrophe, sickness into a triumph. They called her "Mother Miraculous" when she would make them squeal in terror as she removed both hands from the steering wheel for a second, as the car sped down a hill. They called her "Mother Miraculous" for always managing to keep them together, always, the family first. Together. Always. "Mother Miraculous" cooking impossible meals from nothing, feeding the cultured taste of the old man who at fifty hobbled like an invalid, broken after the elections. "Mother Miraculous" spun no more magic spells. She spoke hard pragmatic words.

And now, standing there like that, this woman looked incredibly small and very lost. When they had embraced in the room after hearing the news of the death, Ferron had been struck by how much shorter and smaller she seemed than he expected. She had accumulated the weight of childbearing and kept it. Yet at that moment, she seemed tiny.

Ferron thought Clarice would have gone, but Clarice stood still, looking to the front gate. She was expecting somebody. Lucas continued to look at the television. Ferron stood.

When they left the house it was already dark.

Kingston shone like a jewel from the hill. The city lay there, a natural part of the landscape, a lake of lights tucked away in the armpit of the black mountains on one side, and the open blackness of the sea on the other. Kingston glittered, lights chaotically blinking orange in the night. A cool breeze tumbled off the mountain.

Mother had not spoken all the way up the hill. She asked him to stop just above the parade ground in Newcastle. She climbed out of the car and walked a few yards away. He could hear her singing an old song his grandmother, her mother, had sung for them the day she was leaving for England. Mother's voice trembled in the cold. Then there was silence. She prayed. It began with her Hail Mary, uttered slowly. This was the journey back to faith, back to the days in the convent school she attended as a child, where the Irish nuns taught faith in Latin. Then her prayers assumed the cadence and tone of her mother's Pentecostal utterances. Christ was sitting before her listening to this intimate prayer. Ferron could not hear her words, but she spoke casually. Then she ended with another song, this time something Lucas must have taught her. It was one of those new charismatic renditions of a psalm—composed to sound Jewish in rhythm and melody.

She returned to the car and sat down. They stared into the night. He knew she was thinking about Lucas and what he had said. Maybe they did push the old man, maybe, but he was dead long before that. Ferron knew that this was what she wanted to tell Lucas in the room, but could not. He had died and they had killed him, killed his desire to continue, his dignity, sapped everything from him. At his bedside she had asked him why he did not fight harder, but she knew the answer. All he had left were his dreams, his much repeated fictions of things to come.

"He was going to take us back to Oxford. Those were very green days, Oxford. Very green days, eh?" She spoke in that same distant voice. "He was always a dreamer, that man."

Ferron could feel her smile glowing against the side of his face.

"You keep the ashes, okay?"

"Yes."

"Delores." She paused. "She still won't let you . . . ?"

"I don't think it will work out. It's this country; the fear. She keeps thinking about it, you know." Ferron knew he was preparing everybody for something he planned to do.

"She needs your support," Mother said, turning to Ferron.

"I know."

"Sometimes it takes awhile, you know."

"She thinks I should have done something." Ferron had not said this to anyone, but he knew it was a good time. "She would never come right out and say it, but . . . She keeps . . . She keeps at me now. Can't do a thing right . . ."

"Takes time, sometimes," Mother said. Her voice trailed. She had returned to the old man.

"Yes," Ferron said, ending it.

Mother kept looking out. Ferron heard a car coming up the hill. He remembered their vulnerability. He was thinking of the fair-skinned one who kept his gun tucked away, the one who said: "Believe you me, it real as hell, an' 'member, Cato don' tek it out unless it mus' use, de ting too damn heavy." Cato used the heavy object to knock him to the ground, his head bleeding. He could hear Delores and Cynthia screaming even when he was still unconscious.

Ferron started the car. They drove down the hill with the radio playing old rocksteady hits. Mother hummed along. They entered the sordid belly of the jewel.

Unpublished notes of George Ferron Morgan

The deputy editor is obviously a newspaperman, skilled and knowledgeable, and I do not understand why he was not made editor, or rather, I do understand. He is a pleasant man and he holds the paper together whatever the assistant editor might suppose. He is younger than the assistant editor, which must add mightily to the a.e.'s gall. The Star editor is the saddest case in this office. He has massive experience in the news world but there are two things against him—he is not a Jamaican and he is not a university man. He drifts and that publication reflects a mind that has serious philosophical concerns; but he is politically ambiguous. Perhaps that is a healthy thing, but those types disgust me.

There are three men who run around the office. I do not understand why it should be necessary to run if you plan your day properly and allow for the unexpected. The most remarkable runner is not in the editorial office. He is a Rhodes Scholar (president of the Oxford Union in his fourth year—his scholarship was for three years) who seems to be trying to catch up with himself. He occupies an office on the fourth floor (where the managing director, a pleasant man, rules) and is editing a directory of directors—the ultimate, on the face of it, in snobbery. It is the easiest and simplest of jobs but he has built it into a task of Hercules. He is director of special projects who gets nothing done. The Rhodes selectors obviously made a mistake, as they sometimes do. The other runner is the news editor. He seems an experienced man who never dreamed of becoming news editor and he, too, is catching up on himself and clearly does not plan his day.

He forgets things—bad in a news editor. The third runner is the office manager, who is straight out of Dickens (he would be delighted to hear this). He is obviously imitating, in speech and smile and the nodding of the head, some ancient white worthy, and as office manager he has so much work to do that it is an effort to keep up. He is particularly concerned about crumbs of food around the office.

I am intrigued, at the tail end of my life—for it has to be the tail end—with the problem, which everyone faces in this open office, of how to appear to be working for eight hours a day. You can be seen by everybody. The dodges are transparent. Should it not be a rule in a newspaper office that if you have nothing to do, you should read an approved book? This would probably add more to the good of the country than the misrepresented news. But no, the telephone is the principle dodge—that most unreliable instrument—and the news is further distorted. I hate using the telephone to try to get accurate information. Information should be typed or printed or handed out.

(Incidentally, the office manager can hardly be efficient. When I arrived it took him a week to get a typewriter for me and he has not yet found any keys to my desk. Again, he makes his judgments on the status of the red chair. He must save the company a lot of money, but you can be sure that he won't get any of it when he retires.)

TEN

The next morning Ferron went down to the funeral home to make arrangements for the cremation. Clarice drove him down. She wouldn't pick him up afterward as she had some business to do in Ensom City. She would not evict her tenants; they paid the mortgage; instead, she would move in with her boyfriend's family. They lived in Mona. People would understand.

"You should take a cab out," she said, stretching across to lock the passenger door. "This place looks kinda dangerous."

The sun was directly overhead, beating down. He watched her maneuver her Datsun past two huge speaker boxes set up in the middle of the road. A group of children played "scrimmage" with a stuffed-up orange juice box outside the funeral home. The entry of the building was guarded by a wrought-iron grille painted gold. Inside was a tinted-glass doorway with the words *Abrams and Son Ltd* painted in a golden arc in bold Gothic lettering. The paint was peeling. To the side of the building was a solid black iron gate, open on one side. This is where they had backed the Volvo to deliver the body the week before. Ferron walked by the gate looking in. He could see the small chapel tucked into the far end of the courtyard which was shaded by the interlocking branches of several mango trees. A fair-skinned man, with a jungle of light-brown hair, sawed a plank on a workbench in the middle of the courtyard. He glanced at Ferron and then continued to saw. Sawdust and leaves covered everything.

The children scattered as he neared the door. The grille was unlocked. He pulled it away and pushed the inner door open. It was cool in the office.

She smiled constantly, this high-brown woman with wispy gray hair who fidgeted a lot. Ferron thought of the man in the back. Her brother or her son? They looked alike. The man was lighter-skinned, but the heavy foreheads were identical.

"I am the son," she said, her voice high and lilting in that St. Andrew middle-class accent. He did not get it. "The sign: *Abrams and Son*; I am the son," she laughed.

Her colorful dress strained against her bulk, uneven at the shoulder. She kept pulling it at her stomach. The dress would roll up again whenever she moved. She kept a pink handkerchief tucked into her heavily powdered freckled bosom, which she pulled out to wipe her palms whenever she had to write anything.

"The boys didn't like the business." She fidgeted with her skirt and then her gold-framed glasses that rested on an angular nose. "It takes getting used to." Removing her glasses, she dabbed her face. Ferron noticed a thin green vein that curved down the bridge of her nose and vanished into her cheek. She looked quickly at the kerchief to check for makeup. She smiled up at Ferron. He was still standing.

"Sit, sit, man," she said, waving him to the chair. She bent over, disappearing behind the huge black desk, the kind of thing that could sell as an antique. Piles and piles of paper were strewn about it. "Morgan, right?"

"Yes." Ferron could see into the courtyard. Occasionally, the tangled hair of the fair-skinned carpenter would bob past.

She emerged with more paper. Light, piercing through the trees, caught her glasses which kept shifting up and down as she read the papers which she now held in both hands. Occasionally, she would swing around in the squeaky black chair to look into the driveway. The room smelled of rosewater and lavender. She started talking as she passed him form after form to fill. Ferron worked quickly, trying at the same time to nod, as if he were listening to her.

"Oh, we go back a long way." She was talking about his father. "He wouldn't remember me, but I remember him. Cricketer. Oh yes. Boy in his whites and blazer, child. They would strut. In those days, boys were gentlemen. But if you asked him, he probably wouldn't remember me. Ferron Morgan. Hurt me so bad when I heard. Yes . . . that one too." She pointed to another sheet of paper. Ferron signed.

"Vineyard Town." The chair squeaked as she leaned back. "That used to be a residential area one time, you know? Oh yes. But these people start to move in there in the late sixties. Any and anybody. The place is virtually a ghetto now. I mean, I should know, our place is still there and those people are a real worthless set a tenants. But tell them that, nuh. Tell them and them liable to just shoot you. And people say it's our fault for moving out. We had to move. Had to. You notice how it is with Kingston, now. The ghetto, it moves. Now it reach Half

Way Tree and still moving. Five years ago, we had to get city council to put up a big wall right in the middle of my street in Barbican. At least it's safer. They know not to come beyond that point." She stopped talking and turned to look through the window. Ferron stared at the pictures on the wall. The old man, her father, was darker than she was. He sat in a black suit with a cane in one hand and a pipe in his mouth. In his other hand he held his gold watch. His eyes looked faded. Patriarch.

She turned around.

"Do I have to fill in everything?" Ferron asked.

"'Fraid so, unless one of my people did it, but you wouldn't trust them. They buried the wrong person once. Not a lie." She laughed. "Sometimes you have to laugh at these things, you know?"

"I suppose." Ferron continued writing.

"Your grandmother was Morgan, nuh? Yes? She lived there, just her alone. Nobody else . . ." She paused, waiting for Ferron to help. He didn't. She continued: "Well, a nice lady. A teacher. We buried her. I think Papa did her himself. Wouldn't let anybody else touch her. My mother said black people sometimes don't really know how to fix the white faces. It can be an art. For him, it was an art. For me, it's just business. Finished with that one?" She took the sheet, and pushed another in front of him. He was filling in the same details: *date of birth*, *place of birth*, *date of death*, *place of death*, *relatives*, *funeral chapel*.

"It's the same information," Ferron complained.

"You will thank me for this, dear." She sounded like a schoolteacher. She looked at the form. "Born in Nigeria? Oh yes. I remember now. She was a missionary, not a teacher. From Africa, right? They came from Africa.

Wait, wait." She got up and hurried out of the room. As she moved past Ferron he could smell a thick, sweet mixture of sweat and perfume. He stopped writing and watched as one of the hearses drove in slowly. The gate was locked.

She came back in with a black folder overflowing with old newspaper clippings. She sat behind the desk and began to rummage through, quickly. "I am sure I put it here. We like to keep records. It is here . . . Oh, this goes so far back. Henriques; you know the Henriques family? We did the grandfather. Nice man." She continued to search. Ferron wrote.

Last known address: *Unknown.*

Occupation: *Former university professor.*

Last employer: He started to write *Vera Chen*, then erased it. Instead, he wrote *self-employed.*

"Here it is. Look, look." She held up a large clipping from the *Gleaner*. He reached for it and she pulled it back quickly. "Oh, sweet savior, it's your grandfather indeed. Spitting image!" Then she let him look at it.

A man dressed in a thick black suit and tie smiled broadly into the camera. Clean-shaven, his face was barely distinguishable because of how dark he was. Ferron recognized the nose, the bulbous eyes, but the animated smile was different. The man looked happy. He held up two elaborately designed West African shields. In front of him was a table of assorted sculptures, masks, material, tools, and weapons. Beside him was a light-skinned woman, short and very thin. She was dressed in a frilly white dress. Her eyes were closed. She held the pelt of a spotted animal away from her body as if trying her best to ensure that the camera captured it. The caption read, *Reverend and Mrs. Morgan, of St. Ann, display African artifacts from Africa. The Morgans are missionaries who have returned from the "dark continent" with good tidings.*

This was the second picture of his grandfather that Ferron had seen. The other was a faded and water-stained photograph taken outside the old house in the St. Ann hills when the old man was just a baby in a dress. The flash from the camera had dilated his grandfather's eyes. Ferron always noticed his gnarled right hand clenched in a fist. The left held the narrow handle of a cricket bat. He wore a straw hat that was firmly set on his head. Ferron had always thought it odd that he was about to play cricket with a bow tie on. But those were the times.

In this photograph, his grandfather was a younger man, and his gaze was softer—there was something hopeful and almost restless about his smile. Ferron kept staring at this strange photograph, trying to make contact. The woman reached for it and pulled it away from him. "Wait," he said, taking it back. He wrote the details of the newspaper on a sheet of paper that he stuffed into his breast pocket.

"Missionaries. I tell you. This exhibition. Oh, we went. Hundreds and hundreds of things they brought. Stools, sandals, everything. The people were so grateful to your grandparents, they gave them everything. We have done a lot for Africa, you know. People don't know that, they just don't know." She smiled. "Never seen this before, eh?"

"I just don't have a copy," Ferron lied.

"I like to do this. Bring people back. Sometimes I put on the gramophone and play some of those old-time songs from the thirties and forties, and people just sit here and cry. Sometimes they dance, especially the older women. They like to remember how the men used to be, young, carefree, healthy." Ferron had finished filling the forms, but the woman wanted to talk. He sat back. She leaned forward. "Some people think it is strange, me, a woman, doing this kind of business, but it is the most natural thing. I think it is good for a woman to do the business, because only women really know. It is a gift from God. Once I had a couple here—well, the man was dead, and the girl wouldn't eat and she was ready to just die. When I finished with her, she was laughing and dancing, and we ate dinner right over there where we have the coffins. Most people just want some mothering, you know. Most people want to have nice memories, funny memories. I can do that. Look and me and you now. I gave you something special, just like that, and you feel better, right?"

Ferron nodded. If he indulged her, she would stop.

"My father couldn't mother. People came in here and the place was dark, and they would walk out bawling and bawling—which is bad for business, because people hate to spend money when they are sad, eh?" She gathered the papers he had signed. "Cremation, right?"

"Yes. On Friday," Ferron said.

"Yes. Cheaper. Simpler. Some people feel funny about the ashes, but they don't have to keep them in the house, you know. Some people just bury them—we can arrange that . . ." She waited for Ferron to request it. He was silent. "Some just throw the ashes away. Spiritual thing, eh. Anyway, it is cheaper—we don't burn the clothes, that way you save a good suit. Just underwear. And then, after that . . . it's finished." She looked at him as if trying to read his mind. Ferron stood up.

"Can you show me the coffins?" he asked, tucking his shirt into his pants. His back was wet with sweat.

"You don't talk much, my son," she said, walking around the desk pulling at her dress. He could see her white slip. "That would worry most people, but you must understand that I spend a lot of time with people who don't have a whole lot to say." She laughed heartily at her joke, completely unconcerned about Ferron's blank look. He respected her for that self-assurance.

She led Ferron through the dark corridor lined on one side by a row of caskets with plush velvet linings and well-varnished finishes. They were locked behind a thick, black iron grille. On the left was a raw plyboard wall stained with huge brown blotches. Through a doorway, he could see a group of simple wooden caskets; unadorned, unvarnished, and empty. She did not show those to him. They walked along the tiled floor. She opened the grille to show the display of coffins.

He chose one with a white inner lining. He had wanted to chose the cheapest one, which looked just as good, but she would have been embarrassed. His father belonged to a world that she thought she knew and understood. That world was made of people who would be buried expensive.

"I will show you the chapel. I know you picked a place already, but in case, you know. The larger churches can charge a lot." She was already walking toward the other end of the building. "I am very proud of it."

They were in the back compound which he had seen from the gate. It was colder there than in the coffin room. The chapel was a makeshift altar, a podium with a huge Bible on top, and several pews. She called the man with the hair—Alphonso—to come and tell Ferron about the chapel. He spoke in a dry monotone, repeating with a slow, painstaking care the history of the chapel.

"This year make it fifty-five years. All kind of people buried here. Rich people, poor people, politician, professor, lawyer, and," here he slowed down and thought, "leaders of the churches from all denomination. To bury here, you can make arrangement and we will even provide a minister. If you want, some of our people will witness the ceremony and it will be done in a God-fearing way. No hearse not involve, no whole heap of flowers, we have these," indicating artificial flowers, "but can order good one for you . . ."

"Some people prefer the real flowers. Symbolic, you know," the woman added like a school mistress. She smiled for Alphonso to continue.

"Arrangement mus' make beforehand and we will kindly inform you of plans. We can make program if you want."

Ferron was uncomfortable. Alphonso looked to the ground. "Thank you," Ferron said.

"Thank you," the woman said.

"Thank you," Alphonso said, and sloped away.

"One of the rewards of my husband's waywardness. Pity, eh? With skin color like that he coulda gone so far," she said, shaking her head. "Drugs. Drugs. Mash him up. But he is the only one who interested in this place, you see? Maybe he will learn. Maybe."

She was suddenly extremely quiet. A heaviness fell upon her and she led him back to the office, wiping her hands with the kerchief. He made a down payment. She thanked him. She promised to be at the funeral. They shook hands and he noticed the age in her eyes. Beneath the mascara and eye shadow was a maze of wrinkles. Ferron wondered how they would do her when they buried her.

Outside, the sound system was blasting out dancehall music into the street. A teenage girl stood in the middle of the road dancing in the sun with her tiny shadow as her partner. She stared down into the ground, swaying and bopping in one swoop of motion to the "water-pumpy" bounce on the speaker box. Her rolling body undulated crazily on the unruly asphalt strip. Her eyes turned downward into herself, as her head, laterally steady as if held by a vice, nodded to the music. The rest of her was a dreadful beauty of circles, coming close to a disjointed climax. Her youth, her ability to disappear into herself, oblivious to his staring, impressed him. After Mrs. Abrams's darkness, this sweating, this lively act of "shocking-out," was like breathing.

He thought of Mitzie as he stared at this display.

It aroused him.

Ferron walked slowly up the street. The heat caused his armpits to itch with sweat. He was startled by the screech of tires. Jumping aside, he watched a white Toyota race past him, the heads of four men darkening the inside of the car. The vehicle turned sharply at the top of the road. It looked like the same one he had seen the day before. He stood still, his knees trembling with the shock, his entire body itching. Just as suddenly, the street was empty. The music from the system, with the requisite announcement of a tight drumroll, shifted to a syrup-slow, sticky reggae.

Unpublished notes of George Ferron Morgan

. . . *There is a reference library. They keep clippings in envelopes, untidy, very scrappy, and hardly the kind of reference material one can use with speed. Everything depends on the intelligence and learning of the people who make the clippings, and they seem to be deficient in both of these qualities. There is a clipping file of murders. It is the best-kept file. A thick folder with story after story of murders. I sometimes forget just how bloody this place can be. We kill so routinely. Of course, think who is murdered. The violence is so selective. Most of us live in fear that one day the killers will realize that the implications of murdering a politician or some big shot have been exaggerated. They will know that we can't do a thing about it, and when they do, we will all enjoy a sweet and rich paranoia.*

Were I in Africa still, I probably would be dead. Maybe that is an exaggeration, but I would have no silly delusions that that file of clippings has nothing to do with me. When word came that the military tribunal had decided I was something of a nuisance, I knew they were telling me that I could die. Be killed. Of course my comfort here is nonsense. I am nothing, here. I am nobody. If anybody doubted that when I had a job, now they don't. The election is over; I am nothing. I have no friends in high society. I can be done away with. My one comfort is that such a death would be heroic. But I am not even worth that kind of death. I am now silenced. Only revenge or the pathology of crossing t's and dotting i's could justify anyone making the effort to kill me. Maybe some people are bitter still, but they must know that I did so little to harm their lives. Still, there are those neurotic types—the ones who believe in completing things started. For someone like me still to be walking around is just untidy. Maybe I will be a clipping.

You can get clippings but not the simplest information like the name of the librarian of Parliament. One chap there is a graduate of UWI and is a genuine poet. Strange, I met him some years ago being touted as a poet by Rupert and he was viciously anti-communist. He is now, without much precision, on the left and is tied up with the PDP's new publication which he sells in the office rather like pornography. He has a good mind which, the editor says, makes frequent visits for treatment to Bellevue. He should leave this country for a while.

(I have bashed away at this typewriter since eleven o'clock this morning, without a break, and it is now a quarter to five. The Gardens' people at "Action Station" jabber on and my concentration gutters.)

I am sick and tired of politicians' voices, so drawn up, so insincere in the effort at sincerity. Few of them, in this country, speak English. It is remarkable that they are turned out in print in a reasonable, legible way. My desire at this end of my life is to listen to and speak to only upper-class Englishmen or Africans. I am not depressed but some of this sharpness is a result of the apparent bitchiness of this office. Perhaps their awkwardness is really due to personal insecurity. But for people with secure jobs that they enjoy doing, they behave very strangely indeed.

"What's the Latest?" is a complete flop. It is not what the MD wants and is therefore a nonstarter. I am now being required to do "investigative reporting." Can this be what it seems? Scandal is an essential element in this kind of reporting. It frightens me. With a byline in Jamaica? A profound degradation. At the simplest level, one needs a car and one needs to be exposed always to people one despises or is indifferent to. How many months?

ELEVEN

Everybody came to the funeral. Cars everywhere—
not just cars, but long, black, sleek vehicles.
Suits intermingled with dark lace, blacks and
deep mauves. Hats floated on the green lawn in front
of the square gray-bricked chapel. It was an event. The
sun softened the day; a late-afternoon breeze swooped
down off the Blue Mountains onto the campus. A few
students looked into the chapel, curious about who was
being buried. The prime minister smiled, shaking hands
with everybody. The Frats, five men in badly cut white
tuxedos, sang a madrigal, smiling all the way through.
Lucas accompanied himself on the piano, singing "Nobody Knows the Trouble I've Seen" with a long jazzy
solo which the old man would have liked. He must have
made up with the Christians for a group from the church
sang with him. They were good.

Ferron had suggested he read a passage. Lucas did
not want to read. Ferron read the passage.

Few people were crying. Ferron noticed two; they
were hard to miss. His father's close boyhood friend, Rupert Jones, and Delores. Rupert Jones's weeping made
some sense. According to the old man, they had been
friends through Jamaica College where they shared the
sometimes strained position of being from the rural
lower middle class—scholarship boys. Old Man Ferron

had managed to use cricket to endear him to the wealth-
ier and light-skinned boys, but Rupert, according to the
old man, had resorted to humor—a dangerous clowning
that was always physical and that constantly made him
seem the buffoon. Most of the time, though, the old man
had defended him against bullies, against those who felt
he needed to be turned into a manly type, instead of
the effete boy he was. The old man took him to parties
and clubs and was never ashamed to be around him. He
was, though, a genius. They had been at Oxford together,
Rupert on a Rhodes, and the old man hustling his way
through.

Ferron knew Rupert as a soft-spoken, small man
with an obsequious smile and a hard-to-believe concern
for every detail of his life. He would ask about school,
ask about his health, ask about his diet, ask about just
about everything. It made Ferron uncomfortable. But
Rupert's most annoying quality was how he seemed to
remember details about his friendship with the old man
that always made the old man seem like a helpless bun-
gler, while he looked like his rescuer. "He would have
starved at Oxford, you know . . ." All this said with a soft
quality of pity in his voice. Ferron could not understand
why his father was friends with this man. His reputation
around the university was that he was probably gay. Ferron was impressed by the old man's openness to several
gay friends, but this was a decidedly odd one. One day
Ferron asked the old man, "What is what with Rupert
Jones, anyway?" The old man responded as if he had
been waiting for the question. First he had recounted
the story of their school days, and then after skimming
over the years after Oxford when they lost touch while

Rupert was in the US practicing medicine, he explained why he regarded Rupert as a comrade, as a true revolutionary. This seemed unlikely, but it was what the old man said. Rupert Jones had spent three years in the bush with Mugabe as a field doctor during the war in Rhodesia. He had been wounded, but he stayed on. The old man arranged for his return to Jamaica when he became too frail to continue in the bush. The war was still in earnest. The old man arranged for a teaching position at the university hospital, training students in trauma and emergency medicine. This impressed Ferron. But watching him weeping, a deep moaning sound coming from his throat during the funeral, his kerchief constantly on his face, and his right hand patting his thigh while he kept interjecting, more loudly than seemed appropriate, throughout the ceremony, "Poor George, poor George . . ." it all seemed so pathetic to Ferron. So pathetic.

The other noticeable weeper was Delores. She sat on the balcony with her family. Clarice had suggested she sit with Ferron, but she declined. During the ceremony, her sobbing floated down from the high balcony. Ferron could not quite understand it. She knew the old man, and they got along fine, but they were not really close. Was she crying for Ferron? Or was she simply establishing her role as the fiancée of the bereaved? If that was what she wanted to do, then why had she not sat with him. Of course, he really had not wanted her beside him. He felt this even more when he saw Mitzie. Mitzie came in a simple knee-length black dress. She wore black stockings and clipped along the shining tiles in high-heeled shoes, her bottom rolling easily. He looked at her stomach. She was still showing, but she carried it well.

They did not speak. She just smiled at him. Two young cousins sat beside her. Ferron thought she was staring too hard at him. He liked it.

The three ambassadors, including the old man's writer friend from Nigeria, arrived together in full colorful regalia. They poured libation at the doorway and then strolled into the chapel nodding to the left and right as their sandals slapped the tiles. People whispered. Femi, Nigerian and self-appointed delegation leader, was a handsome man with streaks of gray in his hair. His eyes twinkled when he spoke. He walked a few paces ahead of Kamau, another Nigerian with sharp features and slow eyes, and Quackoo, a squat Ghanaian whose plump face made him look too gentle, gentler than he really was. None of them smiled. They were mourning a dear friend.

After the ceremony, the hearse took the old man away. No one wanted to attend the cremation. Rupert Jones, eyes bloodshot and still sniffling, came up to Mother and embraced her. He did not speak, he just held her hands staring in her face. Then he turned to Ferron: "I should have done more for him. He helped me, you know? I should . . ."

Mother spoke softly, "It's alright, Rupert, he knew you were grateful, he knew . . ."

Rupert Jones walked away after saying thank you to the entire family. Mother said goodbye to the coffin at the church door. She too cried as she tried to thank those who came.

Ferron did not hear much of what was being said to him. Everything was contained in tired clichés. He nodded, and tried to look properly bereaved until the dignitaries had all filed out, jumped into their slick cars, and sailed silently out of the graveled driveway.

Mitzie stood leaning against an off-white pillar outside the church. He watched her swallowing the spectacle, the faces, the dresses, the perfumes, then she caught him looking and peered down.

"Thanks for coming," he said, glancing around for Delores.

"Which one she is?" Mitzie smiled.

Delores was still in the chapel waiting for her parents to finish their condolences to Mother. Ferron pointed her out.

"Nice girl. Hips too low, though. Cesarean," Mitzie said seriously. Then she looked at him. "It was nice."

"Yeah?" She was growing on him. "Thanks for coming."

"Why? Nuh you invite me?" Mitzie tried to look offended.

"But you didn't have to come," he said.

"You never have to come look for me at Jubilee," she said, staring hard at him.

"No," he said.

"Right?" She was smiling.

"Right," he said.

"Real nice." She nodded to the chapel. "I like the African dem. You know them?"

"Uncles, sort of," he said.

"Real Africans, eh?" She seemed genuinely impressed.

"Yes. Ghana and Nigeria."

"Proud, though. Proud. Man, Lewis woulda love see this." Lewis was her baby father. A dread. "Nice." She stepped away from the wall, putting her hands behind her and straightening her back. Ferron noticed that she tucked in her stomach. Delores and her family were coming toward them.

"It was very pleasant, dear, very, very pleasant. He would have liked it," Delores's mother, Gilda, said, lightly embracing him. Thick perfume—very expensive.

"Yes," Nestor, her father, said, nodding.

Delores touched his arm. "Are you alright?" It was the first time she had touched Ferron since. She moved her hand away quickly when he looked down at it. She played with her bracelet.

"Yes. Thanks for coming. Gilda, Nestor, Delores," he said to the parents. Nestor smiled sheepishly—he seemed to have grown shorter and thinner since he had retired from the bench. He was aging rapidly, and had the look of a very bullied man. His eyes were red and wet. Ferron thought he was weeping for himself.

Mitzie did not move. She stared from face to face, half-smiling.

Delores looked at Mitzie and then at Ferron. "You will drive with your mother, right?" she asked. "You don't need a lift?"

"No," Ferron answered. "We will be alright. Thanks."

Delores opened her purse and reached for her keys. "Well, see you then. Nice to meet you," she said, nodding at Mitzie.

"Yes, yes," the father said.

The mother said nothing. She just smiled curiously at Mitzie, and then they left.

"Definite cesarean," Mitzie said, watching them walk away. Ferron noticed the short trunks of Delores and her mother. "You know where she get that, eh?" She then turned to him. "So you alright, then?"

"Trying . . . You look great," he said.

"Dress kinda tight but tha's all me could find. Not too short?" she said, twisting around to see the back of her dress.

"No, not at all." He smiled.

She looked at him and held his gaze. She knew he was telling her she looked sexy. "You too bad. I shoulda wear something longer," she laughed.

"Then if you did you wouldn't make Delores know what she up against," Ferron said, still grinning.

"You really feel you are that important to me, dutty bwai?"

"Who knows," he said. He took her hand and squeezed it. "Thanks."

"No problem, baby," she replied with tenderness. "Make sure you alright."

"I am fine," he said. "Just fine."

The chapel was empty except for the three ambassadors. Ferron realized that Mitzie must have taken the bus. "You need a lift?" he asked.

"No, no . . ." She bent over and slipped off her high-heeled shoes and stuffed them into her bag. She now stood just a few inches below him. From her bag she took out a pair of worn leather loafers, tossed them to the ground, and slipped her feet into them. "Nice. Ready now. Give me a shout nuh. The girl want to see you. I think she like you." She leaned forward and put an arm around him. "You must cry, you hear? Cry." She kissed him lightly on the cheek, looked in his eyes, and smiled. With that, she strolled away. He watched her climb the slight banking in front of the chapel and trot across the main road. She disappeared around some buildings.

* * *

In the car back to their home, Lucky Dube's mellow reggae pulsed. Femi shouted above the music, balancing a glass of the libation whiskey. "We should have lined up the whole bloody lot of them and shot them there on the spot!" he shouted. "Fucking hypocrites! That was the prime minister, eh? He looks like a damned prune!"

"At dawn. Line them up at dawn and shoot!" Quackoo, the Ghanaian, shouted back. They laughed. "Let him wave his white kerchief at the sky, let him shit himself."

Femi sipped and shook his head. "Oh Ferron. My brother. They did this to you." His eyes were filling. "We must talk soon, eh?"

"Yes," Quackoo laughed, raising his glass. "Comrade!"

"Comrade!" Femi shouted. And they emptied their glasses. Clarice drove quietly, but she was smiling. Ferron chuckled. These men were like uncles and they helped to ease the burden of Mother's sorrow. Kamau, the most reserved one of the lot, yet the one they all knew had been present at many executions on beaches, drove with Lucas in Mother's car. He had spoken very little since his arrival.

They stood there on the lawn, the smell of white rum thick in the muggy night, with the odd star darting across, staring out and reminiscing as if trying to summon the old man back to another all-night vigil of rum and roasted nuts. Inside, Salif Keita wailed on the stereo. Lucas had gone to his room. Renewed in his faith, he had abandoned smoking again and was beginning to find Femi's constant teasing of his Christianity tiresome.

Clarice had left with her boyfriend for the north coast. She said she needed a holiday. Mother sat on the lawn. She had entertained a few visitors, her workmates and the wives of some of the old man's friends. She offered them food and soft drinks. Some drank wine. Then they left just as darkness started to gather. Theresa had arrived at around seven thirty to see Femi. They had a short but heated argument on the back veranda, and so she withdrew to the white lawn table where Mother was sitting. Theresa wanted Femi to stay with her that night. Femi explained loudly to her that he was in mourning: "My greatest friend, my brother, is dead and you are talking about fucking? What the hell is wrong with you? Where is your decency, woman. Where?" She sat with Mother, thoroughly cowed and embarrassed. She tried to explain that she had cooked for Femi, and that he had told her he needed a place to stay, and it was not like she was suggesting it, and how crude he could be. Then she lamented the death of the old man. She started to drink, and she kept drinking steadily, weeping intermittently, until she was stunned into a still stupor. Mother smiled most of the time, hummed, and stared out.

At about ten o'clock, the men walked past them and faded into the shadows of the tree-filled yard.

The three men stood apart, muttering into the night. Occasionally they would laugh, turning around with their bodies bent. At about midnight, Femi walked away from the group. He was in full white cloth and it glowed in the moonlight. He raised his arm and began to speak. Ferron did not understand the language, but there were constant references to Ferron, the old man. Femi dipped his hand into a bowl of ice water and threw sprinklings of it around. He looked skyward, muttering as if in prayer. He sent another arc of water.

Quackoo and Kamau nodded reverently. Nobody moved.

Then Femi took the unopened bottle of rum and broke the seal. He let it spill onto the lawn, once, then again, and again. With each pouring, he made a fresh incantation. Then he put the bottle to his mouth and drank. He passed it to the others. They drank. Ferron let the liquor touch his lips. He held it. Kamau noticed that he was uncomfortable and took the bottle from him.

Femi took off his sandals and walked farther away. He was talking slowly now, and nodding. The words were barely audible. He was there for about five minutes, talking, sometimes laughing. The other two nodded knowingly. Then Femi wrapped his cloth around himself and walked back rubbing his bare feet in the grass with a look of peace on his face.

"My brother," he said, his eyes glowing, "we will miss you." This he said turning to face the darkness. "We will miss you. And we are sorry."

"They have met him?" Quackoo asked.

"They have met him," Femi replied.

Kamau said, "Amen." And the three laughed.

"J. Christ Esquire!" Femi shouted, and they all joined him. "J. Christ Esquire!"

Ferron laughed with them. Mother smiled and Theresa moved closer to where the men were. Ferron turned to see Lucas standing at the front door. He was not smiling.

"You think he understood the Yoruba?" Quackoo asked Femi.

"He always understood it, brother. He just pretended," Femi laughed.

"Yah. I think he spoke Swahili too," Kamau added. They laughed.

Lucas went inside. The strains of Andraé Crouch's gospel "Go Ahead" floated out onto the lawn. The men did not notice. They were still laughing. Ferron saw the light go on in Lucas's room. Mother turned to look as well. The record played until it stuck. Mother went in quietly and took it off the turntable. She let the radio play oldies all night. Theresa kept drinking in the yard. Femi sat beside her.

They drank rum through the night, speaking of the old man with tears and laughter. As the sun came up, Ferron, who had barely slept, found the men sitting in the yard. Kamau and Quackoo went inside for breakfast. Femi winked at Ferron, nodding his head to the driveway. Theresa was sitting in her Accord, waiting for him. Mother came out to see where Femi was.

"You know these women," Femi said to her. "She said she cooked for me. So if I don't go I will be a man of terrible morals and deep unkindness." His laugh bellowed through the silent morning. He promised Mother, kissing her, that he would come back. She laughed and warned him about his age. He winked again at Ferron and muttered something else about women. Ferron wanted to ask what the old man had said out there on the lawn that night. But he was afraid to. The morning seemed so different. The magic that allowed him to believe that the old man had been sitting out there on the lawn, Buddha-like, witnessing his own wake, was gone. But Ferron wished there was a message for him.

All Femi would say was: "We were not the best friends for him, we did not come when he needed us, but he still talks to me." He had said this to Mother early on Saturday morning when the sun was crawling over the hills. The orange lit up Femi's white cloth. "We are here, sister, eh. It is our job." Mother cried quietly. Nobody spoke, they just watched her do what she had to do. She sang a hymn softly and rocked. The men nodded as they had done when Femi was in the bushes. Theresa kept wiping her eyes, but she did not reach to touch Mother. It was not necessary. They all knew that.

Then Mother stood up and walked to the house. Everybody followed except Theresa and Femi, who spoke for a few minutes before he came into the house alone. No one could say for certain whether Theresa left the house. But she was parked outside waiting for him when he woke. The others slept until four in the afternoon.

The question of lunch bothers me. There is my diet but I cannot go on being hungry all day. A new canteen concessionaire is expected soon and there is money involved. One must work something out. Two patties should be enough, and water, but I shudder at sending out messengers. There is a depth of uncertainty. I remember being quite as unsettled as this in my first six months of work when I returned to this country. Much of it was driven away in liquor, but to have known that there were so many really hostile people around made me try to leave on several occasions. What would have happened, I wonder, if I had gone to work with those politicians—perhaps as an advisor? Nothing much more than happened to some of the others, but I would have financial security if I were still alive. These are prudent socialists—they understand the value of investment and the doors that political position can open. Who can blame them, anyway? The pension for a parliamentarian is a joke. I have no stomach for that kind of thing, though. I would have worried about being killed. A silly thought, of course, since none of them are dead. None of the politicians are dead despite the terror we all feel. These gunmen have made a simple calculation: to kill a politician would be like killing a white man in Jamaica. One never gets away with that kind of thing. They will kill me now, though. I am neither a white man nor a politician. I feel no terror. After all, it is the tail end of my life.

It is incredible that they could not have found, by some maneuver, a safe place for me. The job at the university still puzzles me.

They made no appointment. No outsider from the Caribbean would have been allowed in. I applied in 1973. With five years I would have written any number of books and articles. They sat there, my Oxford "friends," the VC himself. At the same time, had I gone there I might have ended up with the left wing of that institution, but I would still be there. Instead, I accepted a lack of security in the confident hope that at some time I would have been able to slide out or be eased, by a sympathetic government, into a comfortable old age. That government was inefficient and unsympathetic. Does anybody realize how very selfish the former prime minister is, how much he dislikes those friends of his who maintained a distance from school? He will punish you for not believing in the myth and for breaking the legend by going to Oxford, for instance, without anyone's blessing or permission. We have a sad country. The new leader is a nobody—from the dry-goods store, no basis in this country, not even his relationship to the Hanson-Bustamante circle, nothing except Harvard (just what is Harvard, anyway?) and some prodding from M.G. Smith (who cannot escape positive blame); but the Jamaican people, who reiterate that they are slaves, will never recover. We, as a people, are quite dead. I look around me and can find none of the promise that I saw in the colonial secretary's office in 1946. They had been picked for color or subservience, but they were going to be themselves, not (most of them) anybody else's man.

But not in 1980. They sold themselves deeply down the drain. Nothing would have happened like a communist takeover, etc. We would have had to go back to the IMF and it would have been a hard, uphill struggle in which everybody would have suffered. Except those who still steal away millions to Miami. There is a kind of middle road which can be maintained with sheer efficiency and guts. The PDP was woefully lacking in those things. But what is the alternative? We still are boggling and we really do not know where we are going—except back to being a colony with Reagan's economy supporting some of us. But we asked for it. No amount of skulduggery could, by itself, have caused that defeat.

You would think that I do not have children who must live beyond this. You would think I cannot hear Bob Marley wailing on the airwaves. You would think I have already decided that I am dead and there is simply no hope. Perhaps there is hope. But I have no idea what it looks like. And yet, I think my son, Ferron, might make something of himself. I worry for him. He lacks dogma. Perhaps that is why he will survive. At least he knows he is an African. That must count for something. He avoids me. As if he fears that I might taint him somehow. I can't blame him.

TWELVE

The one called Cato looked darker in the photograph. His eyes were set deep and he had a beard. The other two, whose names Ferron did not know until then, were the same. Tough, hardened men with eyes half-closed—casual. Typical mug shots. Earnshaw, aka Bullet, and Laidley, aka Fling weh, Tougher, and Marky. All three were dead. Cornered during a raid in Rema, they had run out onto Spanish Town Road, stolen a car at gunpoint, and led a chase through the city, shooting wildly ahead of them and behind them. Finally, somewhere on the Mandela Highway, they were killed. Cato's bullet-riddled body was displayed on the front page just above the mug shots, bullet wounds indicated with arrows. There were wounds under his armpit. His common-law wife, whose picture was also displayed, was suing. She said he was shot while surrendering.

There was a brief mention of the rape at the bottom of the page where they listed the five weeks of "mayhem and terror" unleashed by the three. Ferron read the story several times. He felt nothing. He wondered about the fourth one, the younger boy who kept fidgeting nervously, changing the gun from hand to hand. Every shadow shift was someone coming. He did not say much, just kept biting his lower lip and flashing his bloodshot eyes around. At times he would smile at Cato's witticisms. He walked off with Cato and two others into the darkness with the women. The other stood guard over Ferron, and then with a warning, left after the screaming had subsided. Delores said he did nothing, the boy. Just watched. The article said he was still at large. The police files had no photo of him.

Ferron had sat on a wooden bench in the Matilda's Corner Station staring at the slowly rotating fan. His head was still bleeding. His body was fatigued. He had half walked, half run the four miles from the university to the station, all the time wondering where the girls were, all the time muttering, "Please, God, don't let them be dead." The police had already heard of the incident. The girls, alive, had been through the station and filed a report. They thought Ferron was dead. It was the receptionist, a dark woman with grease-slick processed hair and very red lipstick, who confirmed that Delores and her friend were raped, but alive. They were at the hospital. Someone had brought them in. "Look bad, real bad. I tell them all the time, you know. Don' fight dem guys, man, don' fight at all. Jus tek it—after all, it better dan fe dead, you know."

They wondered how come he was just getting to the station. He tried to explain, dabbing the wound with a kerchief. He started to describe the men, when an officer showed him the three photographs. He nodded.

"Jesus Christ! Again. Cato son of bitch strike again! I know it, man. I know it." It was almost in admiration. He was smiling. "Who the hell we send out thereso tonight? To the dance?" he asked the receptionist.

"Nobody. Is Hermitage Station business, sah. It was at the Union, right? The dance?"

Ferron nodded.

"I know it, man," the officer said on his way back to the office.

Ferron sat unsteadily. The woman watched him closely, as if expecting him to collapse. She did not plan to move to help him. She did not need that kind of excitement. She gave him a hard look, hoping he would understand that she was ordering him not to collapse. "You better go up a UC, master. You can dead from loss a blood too, you know."

At the hospital, Delores kept screaming at Ferron, "Where were you? Where the hell were you, eh? Eh?"

The doctor said she was just a bit hysterical. Ferron was shaken.

"I said it was dangerous . . ." he started, then he noticed that she had withdrawn completely. Her eyes glazed over.

"It will calm her down. The other one is doing alright, now." He knew the doctor well. They had been at the university together. He looked tired and genuinely disturbed. He stood with Ferron as they watched Delores and the friend climb into her mother's car and drive out. The doctor then took Ferron inside and looked at the wound, repeating, "Hell of a thing. Hell of a thing, man."

Ferron felt sweat seeping into his eyes. He blinked at the sting of salt.

"Alright. Take some Tylenol or aspirin. Should be alright," the doctor said, after. "Girlfriend, eh? Fiancée?"

Ferron nodded.

"On the pill, and all that?" He did not look directly at Ferron.

"Yes, I think so," Ferron said.

"Good, good. Not that there would be a problem, but sometimes, you know . . . Complicated business." He stopped with a dismissive wave of a hand. "Nice, though, real nice." The doctor winked. Ferron felt sick.

He took a taxi home.

It was Clarice who asked about the incident in the morning. He said little. Delores's mother called and provided the rest of the details. In that scenario, Ferron was careless and a coward. Ferron thought of the blood he had shed.

There was no further investigation by the police; the case was closed.

It was as if he were meeting figures from that incident after the article appeared. In Parade, a few days later, he was sure he had seen the living boy, sitting on a van staring into the floor, his toes tapping to the rattle of the van. He must have felt Ferron's stare. He looked up, straight at Ferron. There was the blank of nonrecognition in his gaze. Ferron looked down. He was not sure. Then that afternoon, while walking through the medical school, he ran into the doctor friend who had seen Delores on the night of the rape.

"Hey, look, sorry to hear 'bout you old man. Hell of a thing." The doctor shook his head, a grimace on his face.

"Yeah, a freak thing," Ferron muttered. He felt the acid turning in his stomach. It was going to be a longer night.

"Damn country hospitals, man. What it was, a simple concussion?"

Ferron nodded.

"Damn country hospital, man. Somebody was telling me that you people might sue . . ."

"For what?" Ferron started listening again.

"Well, maybe is just better to leave well enough alone, eh? But still, sometimes you have to put some fire up them ass. That nurse should lose her work." The doctor was wrapping up the conversation.

Ferron wanted to hear more. He felt in a daze still, and he wasn't sure he was hearing what was being said. He thought of Lucas and his questions.

"Yeah, leave well enough alone."

"But what did you hear?" Ferron asked. He was trying to sound as if he knew more than he did. "I mean, what is the buzz around here?"

"Usual business, you know. I hear the nurse gave him sucrose or something—to sober him up . . ." He laughed and then made a peculiar sound with his teeth. "Now if the man was alert when they took him in, that would certainly lock him into the coma, and after that, is anybody's business."

"So why give him that?" Ferron felt a wave of queasiness again.

"Hey, you alright? You looking weak, man. You alright?"

"Jus' tired, you know? So tell me now, this business with the sucrose—why give it?" he asked, trying to relax his whole body.

"If him was drunk, you know? To sober him up. Maybe she never believe it was no head injury, you follow? Never check . . . Deadly thing that . . ."

Ferron imagined the hospital at night. The old man had lain at the bottom of the steps for several hours before one of the boys arrived drunk and stumbled on him. According to the owner of the house, the old man was conscious when they found him, just a bit groggy. Ferron imagined the attempts to straighten him out, to send him to bed, and then the blood—maybe it was the blood that made them decide to take him to the hospital —the blood and his dizziness. The night would have been dark—absolutely black with no streetlights—just that palpable darkness of the country. And these strange men carried his father to the car—the last journey of the old man in the arms of strangers, bleeding, his eyes unsteady—life seeping from him. The ride to the hospital would have been bumpy as the two men argued with each other about some woman or about some task to be done. One would have been saying over and over again, "You alright, master? Just try get some res', now, you hear? Jesus Christ. Why yuh never look firs'?" And the older one would be telling the other to shut his arse and drive the damn car and not to crash it with his drunken self. At the clinic, sleeping in the late hours, nobody moving except maybe a guardy shaken out of his sleep, they tried to get attention from someone. The duty nurse came in and saw the three men—one bleeding, the other two red-eyed with rum. She hissed her teeth, and in that slow, nonchalant way of women who are not interested in what they are doing, she led them to a room. They explained confusedly what had happened. She saw drunk men, sent to try her nerves, make her night a trial. The old man answered questions in a slur—age, date of birth, address—everything was answered; Ferron had seen the sheet. She might have heard the polished quality in his diction and his voice, and she might have dismissed him for a man so drunk he was starting to think himself better than his station. The bloodstained bush jacket, the worn shorts, and the slippers on his feet made him look at least careless. *Drunk*, she probably thought. But he tried to answer the questions. He had even signed his name. He was conscious when he went in. Then she muttered something about drunkenness, and injected the syrup of sugar into his blood. Like a man finally finding some peace, the old man, in the presence of strangers, in a strange place, so far away from family, from his children, from his wife, from everything that made sense to him, went into a deep sleep, that coma, never to return.

Standing there in the cool air outside the university hospital, Ferron imagined it, imagined the woman at the clinic, imagined the men, imagined the stupidity, imagined his father's unnecessary death. He trembled uncontrollably.

The doctor friend stared at him. "You not looking good, man. You sure you don' wan' me check you out?" he asked.

"No, I am alright. I am alright." Ferron started to walk away in a daze.

"You need a lift?" the doctor asked.

"No, I alright. Have it arranged. Look, I will see you." He walked with some purpose along the corridor until he was out of sight of the friend. Then he sat on a bench and started to cry. Whether it was the pain in his stomach or the story of his father's dying, he cried. This was something he could not dare tell anybody. The story had a quality of truth to it: a tragic, meaningless, lonely death. Ferron could tell no one about it. He was too tired to find out more, and what would he learn? That the woman killed him? That the nurse and those men could have saved his life, but because they were stupid, because of assumptions, *they* killed him? And who would care? It wouldn't bring the old man back. He sat there and stared into the night.

A derelict dragged himself along the corridor slowly, staring at Ferron with a smile. Ferron got up and moved away. He had sweated until his shirt was wet. He walked quickly before the man could say anything.

He thought of Delores, wondering what she was thinking with the men dead. That evening she called. She had to see him.

"You saw the paper?" she asked.

"Yes," he said.

"Well . . . ?" Her voice had softened.

"Well, what? They are dead. They should be dead," he said.

"Can you come over, then?" It was the old Delores, the old playfully desperate tone. But there was something empty, strained about it. As if she were trying to remember a feeling. "They won't be here. Daddy left for Miami this morning. Mummy decided to . . . go out."

Gilda was screwing around again. It had been almost six months since her last fling. Ferron chuckled. Delores sighed.

"Well, you know how it is with Gilda. And Nestor seems happier than ever when she starts to stray. I must be a complete neurotic, you know." She waited for a few seconds. She was more relaxed. "Coming?"

"You sure it's alright?"

"I wouldn' ask if I wasn't sure," she said sharply.

Then half pleading, "I am not sure about why, nor can I tell you what is going on in my head. It is probably something sick, but I know I want to see you. I want to talk."

"I'll see if I can get the car." He hoped he did not sound hesitant.

"I can pick you up," she said quickly.

"No, no. I think I can get it . . ." He wanted to maintain some control. "Give me an hour."

"An hour?" she said.

"Soon come, alright?"

He drove the long way to her home. The house was in darkness, but the lawn around the house was lit up. The guard let him in.

Unpublished notes of George Ferron Morgan

The level of noise continues. Surely this is the most critical thing here. How can anyone concentrate, think, create in this din? Surely it would be better to divide up the office—there is no heat problem as the place is air-conditioned. Some old-time editor who could not live without the perpetual clicking of typewriters must have insisted on it. My guess is that it accounts for 50% of the faults of this paper. Anyway, I am clicking away in that noise, a futile task. Talk and noise and then the beautiful sound of an old car engine. It is the worst kind of punishment but I must endure it for my family. I must insist on not taking home work from the office. I was able to do this at the Institute even though it meant working long hours. I had better get those figures right. From 7:30 to 5:30 with fifteen minutes for a snack. That is ten hours. My work at home was not Institute work. In later days I worked about six hours, on average, at my desk. I must bring down some books to appear to prepare for the seminars.

There are some others. A lawyer, young and thin; she has no breasts to speak of, but carries something off with her height; she is either cowed by the editor or is extremely conceited. I suspect that she is not a good lawyer but is probably paid an enormous fee to decide whether or not the paper should print. The editor says that there are about twenty libel cases against the paper presently going to court. She must be a UWI lawyer because she speaks English only under stress. Another Trinidadian, married to a Jamaican, who is really the assistant to the editor. She is bright, a UWI graduate, but is losing her charm as the pressure keeps up. She is young and can quite easily get into the money in PR. (Action Station should be boarded off.) She is part of the wider divida et impera played against the editors.

The cartoonist is evidently employed on a salaried basis; at any rate, he lives and has his being in the editorial office. He must have run out of ideas (did he really have any?) because what he does now is read the papers and pick up simplistic things that the poor Merchant Party man might say or think. These, for some reason that is not immediately clear, are printed among the Wants ads. Occasionally he is on the opinion page, but it is certainly not his opinion that is being illustrated. He is a Trinidad white. After I had been in the office for more than a month (precisely after Lowe's piece came out), he came over to me and suggested that Lowe should have been "pictured" with a pipe. He implied that the people (all black) at the Star desk had no imagination. I take it that he knew Lowe from the old days, when Lowe was an artist mostly, painting all those patriotic images and hanging around the Phillips. Yes, he smoked a pipe then. Perhaps it was a little pretentious, but I don't recall it that way. I smoked a pipe too. Everyone did.

A number of columnists come in from time to time. An Englishman, very unattractive-looking—must be Francis Aston. He comes in every day, I think. The editor wanted to offer him a regular job but the question is—where did he come from, is he part of an agency? His writing is most emphatically pro-Merchant Party and anti-PDP, anti-socialist, and anti-communist. The Czech Jew who writes the art column seems to sneak in, whisper to the people concerned with his business, and tries to spy at what I am writing. He has concealed his European name under a pseudonym that is ridiculously English. There is, of course, no improvement in the column: one feels that fine art is disappearing (because of its attachment to Hanson) and crafts are appearing because of the yoking to Sabel. He is a little confused by this maneuver. Cedric Lindo comes in almost every day as he writes so many columns. He does not, of course, recognize me although he might be made to remember, when he was the stringer for the BBC in the midfifties, that I wrote some pieces for him (with my Oxford accent) and that he took over book reviewing for this paper from me in 1955. Roderick Ashman decided to have the duo of Charley Miller and Paul Green, who then corrupted the taste of this country for twenty years at least. Miller also writes "Wormwood" in the Sunday Gleaner, writes editorials in the Star and a column "John Bull" in the Gleaner. He is a most inelegant writer, but no one has had the nerve or the taste to tell him so. The editor wants (should I say wanted) to take over the property, at least read the material selected for the Sunday Gleaner and run a competition, etc., but it would need to be done over Miller's dead body and he looks very healthy: he represents the Pen Club. Anyway, the editor has not mentioned the matter to me again. I agree with Marcus, who has shown a remarkable capacity to survive while everyone else is falling away. It is one occasion where his "tastes" may have helped him to cultivate a sophisticated privacy and guardedness that has allowed him to survive in a hostile world. It must be instructive and sharpening to know that a ten-year sentence awaits you every time you embrace a lover. Still, he abandoned me. But then, we never embraced. I am being a bit cruel. His hunger for self-preservation and his callous ability to allow the bus to roll over me has nothing to do with his tastes. It has to do with being brilliant, being black, and living in this country. He says he thinks that the Sunday Magazine should be an "arts magazine" edited by me. He remains quite generous. It is an art to be kind to the hopeless. Nice idea, but this would mean putting the present features editor (who is really quite sweet and fairly competent) out of a job. Since I am not going to be paid specially for these additional jobs (should I have to stay here), I would rather not see that happen.

The famous columnist Randy Jenkins comes in, usually in the early evening, and makes himself heard. He actually fits into the office like a newspaperman. Bill James comes in from time to time (on *one occasion he did not greet me but I suspect he thought I did not want to be disturbed and not that I might just spite him and do The Natives Are Black). He has been writing for the paper for more than twenty years but is clearly aloof from everybody except the editor.*

The man from the evening paper, who again must have thought that I might work my way into replacing him, phoned the editor to say that my first articles were confused, the kind of joke I don't take seriously. His support for the Merchant Party is paying off in directorships. He is an awful writer. The theater reviewer, Barry Landon, used to limp in until he was hospitalized. The editor said to me, "You write so much more elegantly than Barry." I hope Barry will soon be back so that he can go on reviewing those ghastly plays.

THIRTEEN

"We should just keep trying," she said, her back to him. She was naked. Her skin looked paler than he remembered it.

"What's the point?" Ferron had zipped up his pants. He was sitting on the bed. His fingers played with his shirt.

"Don't you want it to work? It takes time," she said, still looking out. Her hair was bundled up in a bun. Her neck looked thin. Ferron kept staring at her hips. They were low. She had a small bottom. Two round cheeks.

"I suppose," he muttered.

"Look, I'm the one who's supposed to have the problem. I was raped, damn it." She had turned around. "Is me dem rape, alright?"

"Been a hard time for me too, dear." Ferron wished he hadn't been so sarcastic, but he had tried. There was just nothing. No erection, nothing.

"Well, we will just have to keep trying," she said. It was final. Delores had this ability to make every activity seem like business. "Heck, that is what we did best . . . That is all we did." She was back at the bed. She cupped her right breast and began to feel around the nipple for lumps. "I am really horny," she said nonchalantly.

"Does it have anything to do with me?" he asked.

"I guess not. Does it have to have to do with anybody? We all have feelings. Right now, I feel . . ." She stopped talking as she sat down. "I'll get over it. Take a shower. Want to come?"

"No," he said. He concentrated on his body. Nothing. It was the funeral, he thought. Too soon.

"Fine. I will wait till you've gone. Might be noisy," she laughed. "Smoke?"

"No," he said, moving from the bed. It irritated his sinuses sometimes.

"Sorry." She was. She half-smiled with sarcasm, holding the cigarette from her lips. Then she lit it up and breathed out. "You think I am dirty now, right? I was afraid of that."

"No, it's not that. Nothing like that," he said.

"Just a bad night, right?"

"Exactly."

"So we will try tomorrow. How about that? Or maybe you stay the night and maybe in the morning . . ."

"I have to take Clarice's car back," he said.

There was a long silence.

"Come and sit with me. At least put your head on my lap. Touch me. Something." She opened her arms. "Come, man."

He lay in her lap, looking past her nipples to her chin. They remained that way till she leaned forward to kill the cigarette. He shifted a bit. Then they were still again. The radio played in another room. Oldies. Her hand caressed his forehead.

"Sorry about your father. Really," she said softly. He opened his eyes to see if she was crying. She was.

"It's alright," he said.

"It would kill me." She wiped her breast where tears had fallen.

"Yeah." He closed his eyes.

The long silence again. At about this point they would have been on their backs breathing heavily, trying to fall asleep, planning their days. Now, Ferron's mind was on Mitzie. It was all cliché, but he found himself comparing the two.

"Hello? Pleasant thoughts?"

He followed her eyes, then he felt the pressure in his pants.

"Patience is a virtue," she laughed.

She was kneeling on the bed facing the window. He kneeled behind her and tried. It was too soft. He tried to squeeze it in. Too soft. He fell on the bed in frustration, the loose condom flopped over in his lap. She stayed kneeling but turned to him, as if waiting for an explanation. He stared into the ceiling. She got up.

"It's the stupid condom," he said with very little conviction.

"Nuh your idea?" She went back to the window. He heard "Shit." Then she walked to the bathroom. He heard the shower going. He lay back and dozed off.

When he woke, she was lying beside him smoking. He said nothing. She stared into the darkness. They waited.

"I feel dirty, anyway, I don't need you to tell me that. Spoiled goods, isn't that what they call it?" she said casually. "I must be."

He sat up and started to get dressed. She touched his back with her fingers, running them down his spine.

"*He's abandoned me, love don't live here anymore . . .*" she sang, softly.

Fully dressed, he watched her sitting there, her knees drawn up, watching him.

"Sorry for being such a bitch about the condoms, but what does it mean, really? It's nice of you to blame the condoms. But we know better. So let's just continue with that excuse. Let me ask you how long you think the condom will be a problem. How long we going to wait?" She scratched her hair with a long red index fingernail. She used her thumbnail to flick out a sprinkling of dandruff. "I have to ask questions like that, you see?"

He said nothing. He had no answers. It had nothing to do with the condoms. But it had nothing to do with Delores and the rape. Not really. He did feel guilty and he felt as if he was betraying her twice over by being with her now. How could he start to have feelings for Mitzie just when Delores needed him the most? What a cruel person he was not to even be able to try, to make the effort, to hold her, to touch her—even if he could not have intercourse. He could have done what she liked. She never asked, but they both knew that he had not tried and did not want to. And he knew that she did feel dirty, broken by what had happened. He knew that what she needed was his affection, his ability to cut through the nastiness of what she felt and be affectionate. But he was thinking of Mitzie. He was thinking that maybe this was a good time to make the move. He did not need the complication of sex with Delores right now; he hated himself for the thought.

He combed his hair in the bathroom and came back into the bedroom. She was getting a bathrobe from the cupboard. He looked at her hips again.

"You know, your hips are really low. They say it's bad

for childbirth," he said. This was the edge of cruelty that he needed to be able to leave.

"Really," she said. "Got nothing to worry about then, do we?"

Unpublished notes of George Ferron Morgan

An unscheduled power outage prevented me from seeing most of the Let Poland Be Poland show. Orson Welles spoke Donne's "No man is an island" and Henry Fonda read Engels's preface to the Polish edition of the Communist Manifesto. These were odd contributions. I got the impression that the Poles in Chicago must be an election force behind Reagan and the party because he cannot be allowed to stand again. Some of the music was lovely. Charlton Heston (is he Polish?) was a creep. The question is, what about South Africa? Are we not to be concerned about that? Reagan says we must find a compromise. I doubt myself whether there is any real determination concerning Africa. Rawlings has actually made the most significant remark I have heard in years: that if Ghana ever came back to leadership in Africa, South Africa would be finished. It is not chauvinism. Nkrumah would have led to a rapid resolution in Rhodesia or a fantastic compromise.

FOURTEEN

Below Half Way Tree, behind the cream walls of the stodgy Anglican church, stood a large warehouse. Entry to this edifice, which rose nearly three stories, was by way of a flight of metal stairs which led to a green metal door. The windows were all some fifteen feet above the ground. There were worn wooden louvers with black gaps where some of the slats had fallen out. The roof was all zinc, bright in the evening sunlight. Shade trees behind the building rose above it.

On two precariously unsteady wooden posts, about three feet off the ground, was a piece of peeling plyboard on which the words *Stringer Sewing Factory* had been carefully penned in red. Mitzie worked here. Ferron pictured the sewing factories of Victorian England, the sordid sweathouses where women worked themselves to orgasmic frenzies pedaling the manual machines. It was an image from a tattered copy of Victorian erotica which he found in the old man's study. He couldn't shake off the image. Mitzie laughed at his question.

"'Lectric machines, love," she said. "'Lectric."

Ferron parked Clarice's car in the parking area of a paint store. He sat, staring at the entry of the building, and waited. A sharp siren wailed across the swelling traffic on Half Way Tree Road. Then women began spilling out of the small green door. Women of all sizes, ages, shapes, and shades. They moved slowly, chatting, arguing, counting their change for the bus. He was not sure why he was doing this. A part of him felt guilty—as if he was betraying her. But he wanted to see where she worked, wanted to see what she looked like in her own space, casual, unaware of him, as she had seemed in the waiting lounge of the clinic.

Her head was tied with a red scarf which she whipped off as she stepped into the sunlight. She was laughing. Her eyes kept darting along the main road. From where he sat, he could see how her body had changed rapidly after the child. There was still the slight plumpness, but her neck was now long and elegant and her body moved with a fluid, athletic ease that he was not expecting. No one would know she had just had a child. And she seemed to want it that way. She had to keep working, she said, and her mother would have to take care of the child. "Ah love the child, but cyan mek her turn me old before my time, don't?" she asked, smiling at Ferron. He nodded indulgently because he knew she would do anything for her child. At least he imagined this. He had only seen the child once. He had gotten to her place a little early and she was stepping out of the yard to take the child to her mother's place. Otherwise she was careful to not have the child around him. When he asked her about this, she laughed and hissed her teeth dismissively, as if he was just being absurd. He left it alone.

She kept looking up and down the road. She was expecting somebody. One of her workmates waved her hand, teasing. Mitzie shook the tail of her skirt, laughing. The others laughed. She patted her hair and pulled at her slip, lifting her purple skirt at the same time. She wore white sneakers. Her eyes kept darting. Ferron looked up and down the street. There was no car waiting in the dusty yard in front of the building.

The other women waved to Mitzie and continued toward Half Way Tree proper, using their numbers to stall traffic as they crossed, laughing and trotting. Mitzie stood at the foot of the stairs and stared up and down the street.

A tall black man stepped out of the green door. He carried a briefcase. He locked the door and slowly made his way down the stairs. In profile he had the girth of a happy preacher. His forehead shone in the haze. Ferron thought this was who Mitzie was waiting for. They talked. The man nodded, smiled, pointed up the street, and Mitzie shook her head. The man walked slowly away, toward the Anglican church.

Ferron started the car. He was planning to drive by and say hello. There was no real reason for hesitation. They had no obligations to each other, and they seemed to agree that the less they knew of each other's lives, the better. He concluded that he would feel a lot better if he simply drove by and offered her a lift.

Then he saw a white Mazda swing dramatically across the flow of traffic and stop abruptly in the gravel and dust of the yard. Mitzie did not turn around. She was playing a game. The car idled in the yard. Nobody got out. She slowly swung her bag over her shoulder, assumed a businesslike expression, and walked casually to the car. The door was opened from the inside. She glanced around and stepped in. The car stirred more dust as it headed up Half Way Tree Road toward the J.B.C. Ferron followed.

The Mazda danced through the traffic streaming toward Constant Spring. By the time they came to the green of the golf club, Ferron had concluded that the man was wealthy and lived well. He was afraid to know his age. He stopped following and pulled into the Catholic girls' school, cloistered by a rich forest of tall shade trees. He drove slowly over the cattle grids and moved toward the golf club building. He parked under a pouis tree on a carpet of yellow petals. From there he could see the tee-off mound and the long stretch of green of the fairways. To his right was the club pool. He could watch the fair-skinned women, some of them people he knew, lying around in the sun, reading.

This small revelation did not affect him as much as he thought it would. He thought he would be annoyed or deeply saddened. He felt neither emotion. Instead, he felt challenged, liberated, vaguely triumphant—and sexually titillated. He knew that Mitzie liked him, despite her obvious connections, and he enjoyed the luxury of knowing that he was close to a woman with a secret life of somewhat questionable morality. Her secret relieved him of the guilt over Delores. She had already told him about Dave, her baby father. Her honesty embarrassed him. She had assured him that she felt nothing for him. He was simply the baby's father, a moment of abandon at a friend's wedding reception in Westmoreland. They had made love in the van that had carried down about twenty people from the sewing factory. After that, their relationship lasted for two more weeks and then it was over. Her pregnancy did not surprise her, though she had not planned for it. She did not expect support from Dave and got none. He had come to see the baby, and for her, that was enough. He would come back and she was fine with that, but Dave was not her man. He had his own woman, and that was fine with her. Simple as that.

Ferron, on the other hand, had lied. He had painted a picture of complete hopelessness when describing his relationship with Delores. The truth was more complex. He could still marry her, despite everything. He hadn't mentioned the night after the funeral at her parents' place. It would muddy the waters. Now, with this secret of hers, they were somewhat equal.

For the first time in months, his imagination was alive. He tried to picture the man and Mitzie eating together, whispering on the telephone, making love. He imagined the man to be married, middle-aged, and able to lavish her with gifts. He decided against asking her direct questions about the man. Instead, he would spy, he would try to pick up clues, he would try to see how long she would keep the secret from him. Something to look for, to discover, to wait for.

When it was dark, he drove out of the school. There was a message from Femi by the phone. Femi wanted to have lunch. It was urgent. There was another message from his supervisor asking when he was planning to come back to work. He would go back to the Institute in the morning. He went to his room and waited for Delores to call.

Unpublished notes of George Ferron Morgan

I was thinking last night of Jamaica College and I remembered the smells. From the day of writing the scholarship, the smell of that green grass which had just been mowed. Then the green paint of the dining room and the smell of red bully beef and the soft bread that they used for sandwiches. I remember also the smell of linen in the dormitory and the smell of carbolic soap in the bathrooms and the sense of cold water, which was partly smell and partly touch. I recall the smell of candle grease with a tinge of horror that one had not kept awake: that the grease was in your hair, you realized, as you woke up to laughter. The smell of games: linseed oil on cricket bats and the chalky smell of composition balls and then later the smell of leather balls. I remember, too, the smell of the leather of footballs. Particularly the smells of the dining hall: mince and rice, and pork and rice and peas on Sundays. The bread again at breakfast, and cornflakes—which we were brought up on. Beef balls slightly burned, and the sweet biscuits and lemonade at refreshment. But in season, all over the school, was the smell of Bombay mangoes; you could smell it for yards and it lingered. I have a distinct memory of the smell of piano keys in the assembly hall, piquantly because Roy Ashman gave me permission to play the piano when I was still in the junior school. I had not realized, before last night, that one could remember smells so acutely. And they are all smells from Jamaica College. What must have happened is that I started smoking imme-diately after leaving school and the sharpness quickly disappeared. Tastes abundant. I recall the most delicious meal of meatballs and *young potatoes served in a restaurant at the waterfront in Genoa. Roast beef and potatoes in hall in Oriel College with McLaughlin intoning, "Give the potatoes a fair wind, please," taking one back to "Fair stood the wind for France." A fish pie on a cricket tour in Surrey. Lashes of strawberries and Norfolk cream in Norfolk by the sea—they were large strawberries (and cheap) and the cream was impossibly delicious. In Africa, garry and beans anywhere. Fried sprats, eaten heads and all. Of course, palm oil. And, in Jamaica, ackee and salt fish, boiled breadfruit and peas soup.*

FIFTEEN

"I have somebody on that already. Private investigator. Following the followers. A bit rough, but he is good," Femi said, chewing rapidly. "You should try this, man."

"Vegetarian," Ferron said, shaking his head. He was trying to concentrate. Femi was talking quickly.

"Your father, eh, he was a revolutionary. You know that, right?"

Ferron nodded, but thought, *Yes, a dead revolutionary. Look where it got him.*

"You people don't know," Femi continued. "He was, oh. But not here. Not in this country. Never here. Here he became a bureaucrat, a man of simple pleasures. Toothless retirement, he called it. But the fire always follows the warrior. The war always finds him, no matter where he goes." He wiped his mouth quickly with a napkin, looked around for a waiter, and then snapped his fingers.

They had a cool isolated table in the corner of the courtyard. Devon House was expensive for Ferron, but diplomats could afford it. Diplomats and the driven New Kingston yuppies who came in for a meal and expensive ice cream every lunch hour. The courtyard was cobbled with the actual stones of the eighteenth century. Leaves and dried flowers were scattered all over the stones.

"Your brother, Lucas, he is slightly . . ." Femi indicated madness with a circling index finger at his temple. "Too much church. It happens. You have a cousin like that, you know? In England. You knew that?"

Ferron nodded. He wanted to leave. Nobody expected him back at the Institute, but he was working on something very exciting. He had found some more clippings on his grandfather and was slowly piecing a life together. With the dreams still tormenting his nights, he felt he had to do this, this retracing of his past, finding context and meaning. Femi called in the morning and said it was urgent—something about the old man. Ferron was still waiting to hear it. Femi liked to prepare with food and drink. Ferron sipped a fruit punch.

"Try this, man. Here, just a plateful. Here. These are good peas. Good." He poured a few forkfuls into a small saucer. The mixture of vegetables was yellow with spots of red tomatoes. It had come with a layer of melted cheese.

Ferron tasted it reluctantly. It tasted of meat. It was well-seasoned. He liked it.

"Ahhh, see? You don't trust your uncle, eh? See?" Femi said, scooping more forkfuls onto the plate. He called for a waiter again.

"No, no, this is enough," Ferron said.

"Well, more drinks then."

The waiter was already at the table. He took the order and left.

They ate in silence. Ferron was enjoying the vegetable dish. Then Femi stopped chewing and stared at Ferron. His eyes twinkling. Mischief.

"Are you fucking that girl?" He pointed a fork at Ferron.

Ferron tried to laugh away the necessity of an answer.

"What girl?" he asked. Femi's eyes were locked on his.

"The one, ahh, D something. The one with short legs? Are you fucking her? Is that what is happening?" He moved the fork around like a baton.

"Sort of," Ferron said. He looked into his plate. It was empty. He glanced across to another table, wondering if they could hear the conversation. Femi spoke loudly.

"Good. Fucking is good for death. When my father died, I fucked a lot. I cried too, mark you; but I fucked a lot. I couldn't stop fucking. Very strange thing." He looked as if the puzzle of that time was returning to him. "Fucking and death—they are related, you know. I have a friend—because I would never do this—but I have a friend who tells me that he likes to go to funerals when a man has died and left a young woman or a woman has lost her father or a dear uncle. He says that it is where most of his relationships begin, and the women are so open—not just the bereaved, but everyone there. It has a way of opening up the libido." He laughed uproariously, hitting the table with his open palm.

Ferron could not help chuckling.

"Good to see you smile, boy, eh? Eh? Eh? So go ahead. It's alright to fuck when you are mourning. The old man would approve." He laughed, leaning back, scratching his chin.

"Thanks for the permission, uncle." He wanted to tell Femi that they were trying to "fuck" without much success, but decided to leave that issue alone.

"Don't marry her, though." Femi leaned forward. "Dangerous connections. I have heard." He leaned back with a conspiratorial look. "You know, right? They killed your father."

It was Lucas again. Ferron felt the discomfort that had disappeared for the past few days. Now it was back. This theory, this dream of a conspiracy, a murder.

"You don't believe, eh? Lucas told me. No problem. I am working on it. Don't worry." Femi wiped his mouth with the calico table napkin. "Just watch your back with that one. But you know all of that nonsense, eh? Yah. Condoms?"

Ferron did not understand.

"Using condoms. AIDS, my brother! Thousands are dying in Africa from this thing, ah. You use them."

"Yes."

"And after that thing, you know . . ." There was something sadistic about the way Femi said this. So he did know about the rape. Ferron was not certain when the talk of fucking had started. But he evidently knew. "The lumpen can smell them from a mile off."

"What are you saying?" This came with a strong glare.

"Forget it, Ferron. Forget it. I have been jaundiced by life. I am an old campaigner. But I was just talking about general thinkings. We are thinking about you. You should write. Writing is good; it is in the blood. Your grandfather wrote . . ."

"You knew my grandfather?" Ferron was growing impatient.

"The old man talked about him, a lot," Femi said, pretending not to notice Ferron's anger.

Ferron saw the game. Femi relished such games. It was a simple rule and he never faltered on it: a man should be able to stand teasing. If he failed to, he should be teased and teased until he could stand it. Ferron calmed down.

"A lot? Never told *us* much about him," he said. It was the truth. Something that was part of this puzzle eating at him.

"No?" Femi said, picking at his teeth.

"No."

"Hell of a thing," Femi said. Then he looked at his watch. "She is waiting. I hate women who wait. I prefer a woman who won't wait—who does her own thing. Those who wait bring out the exploiter in me. I enjoy, but I don't relish. They do what you want. We get along here, me and Theresa. Perfect arrangement. I come for a week, maybe like now, a month. We fuck like wild goats. Then I go. Just when I am getting tired of her. This is a long trip, but we make it interesting. You have been to Negril, eh?"

"Once . . . maybe twice."

"I like Negril. Rural tourism. Rustic. We are going there. Maybe you should come, with that, ah . . . her name?" He opened his palm toward Ferron, questioning. Ferron noticed the yellow stain of tobacco on the edge of his fingers. Femi had strong hands. He shook hands firmly, almost roughly. He had developed the Ghanaian practice of snapping the fingers vigorously. He always took control of that part of the ritual, roughly forcing the finger of the person he was greeting between his thumb and index finger. Then, the quick, full snap. He once said he washed his hands in a goat's blood to keep them tender. Ferron had pictured human blood when he heard this story, because the men, the old man included, laughed as they always did when they were sharing a private joke.

"Delores," Ferron answered.

"Yes. Delores. Invite her. We could make an event of it. Kamau might come—alone. He is very faithful—to a fault . . . Unhealthy. If you ask me, that Italian wife of his is doing her own thing when he is away. They are very practical, Italian women. Very discreet. Yes, he should come. At least we can have some time to talk. Then we can plot. We have to do this thing properly, you know." He was leaning forward again. "Are they still following you?"

"Who?" Ferron's uneasiness was souring the food in his stomach. Femi's excitement, his boyish enthusiasm, annoyed him. But that was Femi—constantly searching for some diplomatic intrigue to revive the excitement of his youth. It was Femi who called Kingston late one night to announce that he was on the run. The old man had paid his airfare from London to Jamaica. He arrived at three in the morning, grinning from ear to ear. He declared to the family: "I am in exile." The flight was genuine. Three of his colleagues were jailed a month later. Two of them were executed. Femi had escaped. He lived with them in Jamaica for nearly six months. Then he met Theresa and moved in with her. But he would arrive at the house after twelve each night to drink whiskey and talk about the struggle. The old man became animated during that year. He drank more, laughed more, stayed out more, shouted politics through the house more. Femi brought excitement—political intrigue. For a while Clarice was convinced that they were secretly planning a coup in Jamaica. It was during the seventies, and such talk was not unusual. But Femi left. He had somehow got back into the good books of the regime and was invited back to his old post at one of the northern universities.

The old man became sober again and only drank club soda and bitters. Now, Femi was back, trying to make his stay exciting, leaping at the intrigue of the death. *He is writing another play*, Ferron thought. *Another play.*

"Clarice said you thought you were being followed, from Mandeville. Did your cousin Cuthbert . . . Is he the one nobody is sure of?" Femi asked, changing the subject casually. It was part of his style when dealing with political intrigue. Casual. It gave the danger greater weight. "The brother's son?"

"We don't know," Ferron said.

Femi nodded. "It was the police," he said, as if that would make complete sense to Ferron. When it was clear that he still did not get it, Femi continued: "They've been investigating the whole mess from day one and before. Before. They've been watching him. When he went to Mandeville, they were watching him. When you drove back, they followed the car to the funeral home. They went in to make sure it was him. Something funny in all of this, wouldn't you think? She has been having him watched, this Madam Minister Vera Chen. Quite a bitch. She has demons, you know?" He laughed. "Courtesy of Lucas's inside track. Personally, I think she is a man. Ever heard her talk? And she keeps all those women around her. She was a friend of your father's. They were in the same circles. Then, he said, she was a beautiful woman who seemed impervious to the charms of men. Smart, but no dogma—ideologically bereft. She was once a socialist, you know? Well, look at her now. Watch her closely; she will be prime minister before you know. She has it in her—that capacity to order the execution of enemies." He took a long drag and exhaled as he spoke.

"Well, they've been watching the house—your place. They may be out there now, waiting for us. I think that short man behind us is one. Don't look. Watch the eyes. He's been looking. Looks CIA, doesn't he?" He laughed at what he meant as a joke. "I think they've bugged the table."

"You've found out all of this in this little time?"

"Connections." Femi looked at his watch and stood up. He wore a pair of jeans and a light cheesecloth shirt, which was unbuttoned to the curve of his slight paunch. Femi was in good shape. He felt for his cigarettes in his breast pocket, slipped a cigarette between his lips, black with tar. The cigarette bobbed as he spoke. "Time to exercise the back. She can be impatient." He laughed loudly, lighting up. People close by turned around to look. "We should go to the north coast, man. Negril. We will talk better there. Have a few ideas. There will be plenty booze, brother. I have a job to do with you. I promised the old man."

Ferron wanted to ask what he had promised and whether the promise had been made that night on the lawn, rum fumes dancing in the air. He had dreamed of that too . . . the conversation—but it remained vague, a peculiar sensation of longing or yearning with no definite edges, no shape or form.

"Only if you want to, though . . . And bring the girl . . ." Femi was saying, sucking on his cigarette.

"I think she would rather not . . ." Ferron had no intention of making the trip, but suddenly he wanted to hear more about the death, the police, the thing his father had asked Femi to talk to him about, but he was afraid to ask.

"Well, bring anybody. Somebody else." Femi winked. His keys were out of his pocket, jingling. He placed three hundred dollars on the table. "For one meal," he said. "Can't get used to it."

They walked through the inner courtyard, milling with people walking about licking cones. Some had their heads stuck in gallery brochures from the national collection which was mounted in the old colonial building. Bamboo patches spotted the cobbled courtyard in neatly arranged oases. They walked into the bright haze and heat of the parking lot.

"You really think they killed him?" Ferron asked.

"To kill—" Femi stopped as if musing on the issue of killing. "What is it to kill? Your mother says they killed him three years ago. She buried him then. Lucas says they pushed him down the stairs. You've heard that theory. Compelling, eh? And you say he died, he just died—a freak accident. I think you have more faith than Lucas. You believe in freak accidents. That takes faith. Lucas can't reach there. He has found a killer." He flicked the cigarette butt into a neat pile of dust swept carefully to the cement curb in the parking lot. "But you are still angry, maybe with him. Maybe you think he just jumped. Us? We say they killed him. They killed him because they cared that he died, because they were there when he died, and it mattered to them. Because *they* is a necessary construct—a political necessity."

"So you don't think *somebody* killed him?" Ferron asked.

"Aaahhh, now that is a different issue." Femi started to walk. "I had a friend in Poland. Warsaw, I am sure it was. Can't recall now. He was studying there, medicine, natural science, or something—there was blood involved. Who cares? Shit, he was there almost four years, maybe five. Never a bright one, but he went. The people sent him. Hard life, you know? Hard life? Cured him of his visions, you see. The whores were nice, but the women, they read too much *Gone with the Wind*, and Conrad, eh? Didn't like blacks up there at all. Well, one night he goes drinking. He is dead the next morning, my friend. I went to school with him. Dead. They said he drowned in his vomit. Drunk. Would you believe that?"

"If it is true," Ferron said, hesitantly.

"No. You don't. You musn't, because . . ." They were at his car. "Because you have enough fight in you, enough indignation, enough anger at what they have done before, enough imagination, to believe otherwise."

He unlocked the car door. Heat poured out. Ferron could feel it. The inside decor was black.

"I was looking for a shaded area, but . . ." Femi said, peering inside, as if trying to find the source of the heat. "She will have one with air-condition next year." He sat in the car and smiled at Ferron, shutting the door. He rolled the glass down. He had another cigarette in his mouth. "We leave Friday. Give me a call. You should come. Maybe I will convince you to write, or to be a fighter—a true revolutionary. Then you will come with me to South Africa to kill a few Boers. Eh? And bring the girl, Delores. I want to talk to her. Tell her. She knows me."

Ferron watched him race along the serene driveway of Devon House, reflections of the overhanging trees skipping across the slick roof. He drove it hard, as one did a rent-a-car.

Unpublished notes of George Ferron Morgan

I entered Jamaica College with the mistaken notion that I was entering the school of Tom Brown's School Days and the school (Greyfriars, I think) in Billy Bunter's Magnet. My great shock was to find that prefects did not have studies. It took me about a term to recover from this. I was put into 2b in January 1938 and can only remember distinctly that in the term examination at Easter I got 100% in English Language, including a free composition. I do not recall any friends in that first year. We still lived in the country and I went off on my summer vacation pleased with myself at having made the third eleven at cricket. I was a fast bowler. By the third term of 1938, I had made some friends, but two stand out—PL and BE. PL was the nephew of Ethelred Erasmus Adolphus Campbell, a chemist by training but he came to be known as the fighting barrister. My sister seems to have known PL's aunt and he was given the charge of "looking after" me. It was characteristic of him that it took him two terms to find me. When he did he pressed me into service as a courier in his endless verbal battle with Phillip Hanson. I carried the most scabrous messages between PL and Phillip Hanson, repeating precisely what each said. Fortunately, although I was the bearer of quite horrible news, I did not suffer the fate of a Greek messenger. I stopped being a courier when I became captain of the Colts cricket team in 1939. I should have learned my lesson then. Alas, I may have carried far too many messages for Hanson over the last few years. Can I blame people for mistaking me for a friend of his?

SIXTEEN

Ferron sat reading the *Daily Gleaner* near one of the high windows at the end of the library. There were over a dozen huge files filled with yellowing *Gleaners* on the table in front of him. He wrote into a notebook. The fan clunked noisily overhead. The light slanting into the library was tinted green with the trees and leaves from the courtyard. Everything in the Institute's library seemed to be made of dark wood panelling. The wood tiles on the floor glowed. An old man in a light-blue shirt slept at the other end of the room. Mr. Langston was a poet from the forties. He wrote very little these days—just a few sonnets for the *Gleaner* to remind people of his status as poet laureate. It was a title he had won in '43. Ferron found it hard to believe that Mr. Langston was once regarded as a leader in the groups of young intellectuals and artists who were trying to forge a Jamaican aesthetic. Now he seemed archaic, stagnant. He simply slept in the library in between leafing through old copies of the *Times Literary Supplement*. At four thirty, his wife would drive around in their old, beat-up Volkswagen and take him home. He would smile benignly to all the librarians. "Tomorrow, if I live. *In thunder, lightning, or in rain . . .*"

He snored in his tiny corner. Nobody bothered him—they had firm instructions from the director to let him be. Ferron liked Mr. Langston because the poet seemed to know how to laugh at himself. Sometimes, Ferron felt, Langston was parodying the character of an old poet who took himself too seriously. Mr. Langston was the only person who made sexist remarks that Ferron felt comfortable laughing at. It was something more than indulgence—it was a strange realization that this old man would never change. Perhaps it was his frailty, this harmless quality that made some of the female librarians reprimand him with a smile—as you would a child. He would giggle and wink at Ferron. He was what he was and would die that way. Not like Ferron's father, who had seemed to be perpetually in flux. For instance, Mr. Langston, as far as Ferron could tell, would never have an affair. He couldn't deal with the fatigue involved.

Tucked somewhere on the editorial page was the grinning face of Femi. By some clever machinations he had managed to convince the editor, an old university friend of Ferron's father, to let him write a column—a regular dialogue about international politics placed in the context of Jamaican life. When Femi explained it to Ferron, the motives were far less altruistic: he wanted to write five pieces that would, quite simply, "put things in the proper perspective, you know? Let this whole damned country know how they murdered him." Ferron vowed not to read the newspaper for a few weeks. But this was impossible. Femi's rhetoric was eloquent, cutting, stirring, and startlingly frank among the lesser efforts of the long-standing journalists. He would begin with some issue that related to his international connection, which would lead to some narrative that was the occasion for the canonization of Old Man Ferron.

He began the piece about Ferron's father's profound blackness, his Africanness, with a reference to Bahia:

Last week I found myself in Nigeria without crossing the Atlantic. There in the teeming energy of Bahia, Africa was alive. A Yoruba priest talked to me. He was searching for the old ways lost in Nigeria in Bahia! I would not have believed in my blood alive on this side of the Atlantic had I not been tutored by a scholar of Africa, a brother who died in his struggle to celebrate his ancestors in this island. He gave his life for the retrieval of Africa in this place where the colonial masters sought to deny the Middle Passage's living testimony. This is why he died. He died because people are still afraid of Africa in this country. When an Oxford man, a graduate of the best college in this country (a black student at a time when they were scarce), the son of Negro missionaries who went to Nigeria to save souls; when an avowed socialist speaks of Africa, people grow silent . . . Death is not unusual . . .

Femi's poetry threatened to consume the piece. He went on to discuss the politics of Pan-Africanism and the martyrs for its cause. The piece ended with the perfectly intended effect of creating intrigue.

No one will know for sure what killed him. No one will know how he fell; what wind blew, what hand. But many know that in some quarters, some lofty homes ornately decorated with Americana, no tears were shed. You wonder why? We are killing our people, devouring them like mongrels and spitting out their bones to be dried by the blasted wind. "How long shall they kill our prophets, / while we stand aside and look?" The ghetto poet was right. He was very right. It is a shame . . .

Sitting in the cool courtyard of the Institute, Ferron could not help laughing out at the cleverness of Femi's scheme. Ferron had waited patiently for Femi to come to him with more solid evidence that the old man had been killed, that there was something more diabolical about the freak death. In his head, Ferron knew that the nurse had killed the old man. He knew it in a way that gave him some kind of comfort. It offered a narrative for the old man, a truly tragic narrative that was, in a twisted kind of way, quite gratifying. He understood what Femi was trying to do; he understood that Femi was trying to find the means to mourn the old man as more than the mere victim of a stupid accident—picking the wrong door and then plunging to his death in some idiotic and insignificant manner. He also realized that the story about the nurse would not satisfy Femi, for in her could not be located all that was perverse and corrupt about the capitalist society that they lived in. She was probably poor and underpaid, a victim of the system, someone who would not make a good figure of intrigue and tragic consequence. Ferron knew he would not tell Femi about the nurse, not for years anyway.

Femi did come by and offer theories or possibilities. His intention was to suggest that it was possible that the old man mattered enough to the political world that killing him was important. He listed stranger things, stranger deaths of lesser people. In his mind, Ferron realized, even if the death was not a cut-and-dried murder, it was worthy of such status. Old Man Ferron deserved

to be assassinated. He deserved to have been under sur-
veillance, to have been hounded, persecuted, and finally
killed by a system that did not like his politics, his intelligence, his independence, his Africa. Femi's earnest-
ness about all this had irritated Ferron at first, then it
became clear that Femi was working out his own guilt,
over his abandonment of the old man when he most
needed friends. The articles were his guilt-offering, the
myth was his sacrificial act of atonement—the hope that
by deifying the man, he, Femi, would find favor with
fate, with the gods, with his struggling conscience.

Several evenings before, the two had sat in the open-air
cafeteria outside the Creative Arts Centre on the university campus drinking beer in the pink glow of sunset.
They went through a whole crate of Red Stripe. Got themselves completely mellow as the campus grew darker
and darker. The cafeteria was no longer in use—it had
been an experiment by the university to supplement the
meals on the hall for off-campus students that had floun-
dered because of poor management and embezzlement.
The tables had been nailed to the cement floor, so they,
and the inappropriately ornate wrought-iron chairs,
their enamel white paint peeling off to display the rusty
red of the aging metal, were all that remained of the cafeteria. Students used it as a studying spot or as a drinking place in the evenings. It was deserted that evening,
and Femi wanted to get drunk—he needed company, he
said. Ferron had planned to drink just a few bottles, but
when he contemplated the rest of his evening—Mitzie
not wanting to see him, or perhaps wanting to see him
so she could ignore him—the serene cool muteness of a

drunk evening, embraced by the Friday-evening stillness of the campus, this lazy sensation was too tempting. He allowed himself to sit and drink with Femi. Femi wanted them to talk like men, he wanted them to salvage the memory of the old man.

"You look like him," Femi said.

"I look a little like him." Ferron remembered a photograph of the old man when he was a student in England in his early twenties. He was slim, low-shouldered, and rather delicate-looking. But this was an athletic delicacy—the tidiness of a small-framed cricketer—compact, efficient, and fit. Ferron tried to read the smile of this man, strolling down a London street in his tweeds, hands in his pockets, pants baggy and flowing. This was long before he had met his wife, long before Ferron was thought of, long before so much had happened. It would have been about the same year the old man's father had died—blind, broken, and with only the companionship of a wife and the calm of the Holy Spirit at his death bed. The children had been informed, but none could take the time to return. Wayne was drunk and out of reach somewhere in Aruba—he would return weeping and lamenting and threatening to kill himself for having failed his father like that. Ferron's father stayed on in London—going home would have been too expensive; but more critically, going home would have meant breaking the peace of distance, of another world that had so seduced him. In those days, he said to Ferron once, he wanted to forget Jamaica, to forget his father, to forget that he came from somewhere else. Going home would have meant having to remember. He did not want to, so the old man died alone.

Looking at the photograph, Ferron always wondered what regret ate at his father's mind as he strolled through London in those days; what pain was shaping itself in him that would stay with him for the rest of his life. People never really die until you are there to see them dead, the old man had said when his wife was struggling with the question of whether to travel to Ghana to be with her mother. She went, and then mourned for several months, singing old songs and weeping. Then she was over it. The old man said it was because she had been there to see it all. Ferron was beginning to understand this. The sight of the corpse of one's origins is a way, he thought, of facing mortality, of facing one's beginnings and one's end.

"You look exactly like he did," Femi insisted.

"I don't know . . ."

They drank through long silences. Femi looked like a lonely man sometimes. This was one of those moments: sitting there in a strange country with the son of an old friend who belonged to another life, drinking his mind to a numbing calm, not sure where he would spend the night—a hotel room or another woman's bed.

"What did he say to you, eh?" he started again. "Before he died. What did he say?"

"He was in a coma," Ferron said.

"I mean when you last spoke . . ."

"Nothing profound . . . Usual things. He had just burned a steak." Ferron knew this would please Femi.

"He wanted to cook?" Femi laughed.

"He always said he could cook." Ferron laughed too.

"Yeah, yeah." Femi's face glowed, remembering.

Ferron could have told him of watching the old man

reading Joyce's *Ulysses* in his stained shorts and worn, pale-blue bush jacket; his head looking up every few minutes to see through the window to the gate, waiting for the postman's bell. He smoked at least two packs of cigarettes each day, his head in a perpetual cloud of blue smoke, his eyes squinting to make out the words in the tattered hardcover book. This may have been his last novel—the last novel he read—and it was hard to tell why he had chosen that novel of all the novels that lined the shelf. Ferron liked to think that he was doing research for the great West Indian novel he had talked about writing—the great novel that would surpass all novels: the novel that would straddle the diaspora. It would start in Africa, in Ghana, and find its own sense of rooting and place in that ancient soil. From there, the journey would be like that of the harmattan winds to the Caribbean, to Jamaica. He would make a novelistic journey not made by any other writing—a Marxist tome with the sophistication and experimentation of Joyce. There was a great deal of evidence at the time to support this myth. He took notes, always wrote notes in the books and in a pad that remained on a side table by his favorite chair. But no one could find the manuscript— not even a single page that looked like the beginnings of a novel. Ferron could have told Femi of that small tragedy among many. He could have talked about the profound depression that would consume his father when there was no mail, no mail for him. During those last months, he had developed a ritual around the arrival of the postman. He would become impatient when the mail arrived and no one moved to get it. Ferron knew that the old man was afraid to go and get the mail himself—

afraid to admit that he was worried about where his next job would come from, if it would come at all. When no one would go, he would limp to the gate, gather the mail, and slowly walk back to the living room. He would place the mail on the center table and return to his chair, placing the book in his lap—waiting there for someone to come by so he could say casually, "Anything interesting there for me?" But there was never anything interesting. Nothing. No reply to his many requests for jobs, his increasingly undignified pleas to all those friends who "owed him." Nothing. They all became silent. Nothing from the men he had hidden while the army was searching door to door for their hides—while men were being stripped naked and executed by drunken soldiers on the dark beaches. Nothing from the emotionally tormented friends who came to him for shelter and solace as their marriages rotted away or exploded—he was always there. Nothing from the starving writers, now wealthy and well-situated in colleges and universities all over the world—that bunch who would come to him weeping, complaining about their hunger, their thirst, or about how useless they felt, what failures—and the old man would shelter them, spend his money on them, take them out for two-day drinking sprees, just to win them over, awake in them a belief in their sorry selves. Nothing. Not a word, not a reply, no acknowledgment that they had heard from him. The old man said little about those disappointments, but every day his gloom became deeper and deeper.

Ferron could have told Femi that he knew what a broken heart can do to a man. Ferron could have attacked Femi for *his* silence, *his* failure to reply, to offer something. But he chose not to. He just smiled at Femi's tirades about the cruelty of the world, and drank more and more of the beer, until everything became a blur of memory and reality. The dusk created a surreal softness in his head. His mind drifted back and forth.

During those last days, he had a nightmare. It was a dream about himself and the old man. They were in a black cab. The old man was not alive. He was actually dead in the black cab, but they held hands and the car moved quickly through the city. Ferron woke up and wrote a poem about this dream. He wrote about his feeling of calm—the absence of fear and anxiety; the ease with which he seemed able to cope with the prospect of his father's death. It bothered him. There was a time when the death of either of his parents was the worst nightmare that he could have. In his teenage years, he would sit and imagine what it would be like to be without his parents. Once he had so consumed his mind with the fear of their death that he began to cry—just sat there in the garage and cried, for he could think of nothing worse than the death of his parents. Now, there he was, calmly facing the death of his father. It bothered him. But in retrospect, perhaps the dream was a way of preparing him for the actual death—the actual loss. It gave him a facial language, a language of posture and attitude that he could use. It gave a point of reference, a code which, while false, while constructed around a certain unreality, was enough to carry him through the first few weeks after the death. There was, after all, a part of him that saw that dream death as a good thing—as a fitting end to the life of a man who was probably already dead to the world, dead to everything that had meaning for him. It hurt Ferron to think that he had willed his own father, a man barely sixty, to death like he would a man in his nineties suffering from some chronic debilitating illness. But that was the sensation, the thought, a psychic euthanasia. It would haunt him for years after that. It would haunt him that he shed no tears, no real tears, for several days after the news. He said this once to Delores, and she simply said he was in shock. But he knew he was not in shock. He knew that he felt something, but it was not the need to mourn, to weep, to lament with tears—it was a kind of relief. It was hard to explain this to anybody. The only person he thought would understand this was his mother, but it would have been cruel to let her admit this to anybody—to let her admit that she did not see his death as an entirely bad thing; that maybe his dying was a way to end a certain darkness, an uncertainty.

Ferron did break. He broke when he thought of a world lost. He broke when he considered that Lucas could suddenly crumble again, his mind escaping to myth and fantasy because all that was stable and constant was gone. He broke because he felt cheated of a chance to talk to the old man, to really talk to him about adult things. He broke for things that had to do with the living and not the dead. There in the arms of Delores, he had cried and cried and cried for all the tears he had not cried. He cried because he was tired, just completely tired of all the work he was doing. He cried because he did not know how to feel.

Ferron could have told all of this to Femi, but chose not to.

He chose not to shatter Femi's perception of the old

man as the arch-atheist by relating one of the oddest conversations they'd had not long before the death. In those days, the old man stared into the blue sky a lot. He had already accepted the new job out of town, but his heart was not in it. He stared out a lot, nothing less than a look of traveling to another time and place. There were the evenings spent listening to Pentecostal preachers on the radio. Nobody made jokes about it, nobody talked about it, but he kept doing it. Soon he was humming the tunes. Perhaps he had finally become unhinged, lost his place. But were there perhaps new fictions taking shape in his head; new characters, new voices? But nothing was said about it. No one asked. The old man said nothing, but until he left for Mandeville, he listened every night to the Pentecostal preacher, raking hellfire through the muggy Kingston nights.

Ferron stored away these images in hope. Maybe the old man was finding the chapel in the hills of St. Ann where his father preached, where he sang hymns in what he boasted was a perfect bass. Maybe he was returning to another beginning, as if making himself ready, free of vanity, free of pride, free of pretense. Ferron did not know, but he used this story as a way of creating the hope he would see the old man again. Constantly, he would dismiss the doubt in his mind.

Ferron would not say these things to Femi as they drank. Femi had his own memories, his own myths to nurture. They knew two different men; each a peculiar myth, each a stone to regret now. So they talked about sex, poetry, and the Cuban theater. Above all, they drank beer.

It was pitch black when they left the cafeteria. A

power cut had engulfed the campus in darkness. The two men walked to Femi's car with the ratchet alertness of followed men. Kingston's fear seeped into the bones casually, subtly; nerves were alert to the sound of death. Their eyes peeled into the dark, one man taking one side, the other, the other. They said nothing until the car sparked to life. Then they relaxed a bit. The power returned as they turned onto Mona Road and headed to Liguanea.

Femi's articles come out twice a week for three weeks. Old Man Ferron was suddenly a cause célèbre. A group of writers arranged a gala reading to commemorate his death. Ministers stated that they were investigating foul play and it was reported that the nurse who claimed the man was drunk had been transferred from her post for negligence. Femi was celebrated as a champion of a good friend. Femi enjoyed it. Ferron retreated into himself some more. He felt as if he were losing his father, felt that the man was becoming an enigma owned by others. He found himself straining to visualize his father's face; to remember words, ideas, something shared.

Mitzie held his head on her breasts and let him cry a lot. He betrayed the love. He found himself drifting, looking for old girlfriends, finding comfort in their condolences, which invariably became deeply physical. Soon his regret was less for his father and more for Mitzie. At night he would sleep fitfully. Daylight came too slowly.

It was Mitzie's idea that they get away for a while. They had argued about his behavior and his disregard for her. Ferron sought an absolute, complete, and seemingly clear way out: abandon the whole idea of a relationship.

"Chalk it down to my restlessness," he said. "I am no good for you."

"Don't give me that shit!" she shouted. "You think it so easy, huh? You think we could go through so much and you can just use that poor tiny story to mash it up; jus' so yuh can run weh?"

"Alright, I don't love you anymore," he said.

"Yuh think this is a joke?" She sat down on the bed and began folding clothes.

Ferron had thought about it for days. He did want it to be over—the part of him that did not care much for the guilt, the heavy remorse he felt every time she took him in. Rocking in a minivan heading down Maxfield Avenue one evening, he decided that the best thing was to cut her loose, send her back to her sugar daddy, and he could return to his own ways, his own paths. He expected her to hate the idea, but he believed she would go with it. She wasn't one to beg. He had misjudged the situation, thinking he had limited her options to just two simple reactions, reluctant acceptance or pathetic pleading for him not to do this. He was not prepared for her aggressive wisdom, her ability to cut through and clear a path for what she wanted. He could only resort to cheap humor in the face of her aggression.

"So you don't mind my screwing around?" he said, smiling.

"You useless shit, you. You think that you have it set, eh? So you confess to me, right—you tell me how you fail me, how you let me down. Tell me how you not good enough for me so that you own damn conscience will feel better." Her face was calm, except for an uncontrollable twitching of her top lip. "So that when I say you must go on, you can leave free of all you sins, right? Well, no. No. You gwine live with this, you hear? Maybe you don' love me, maybe you just wan' taste a working-class pussy; maybe you feel that now we cyaan profile. You too late now, Ferron. You hear me? Too damn late. Nobody neva tell yuh seh a girl from Maxfield Avenue not taking no foolishness from no man? Dem neva tell you? You listen to me now. If you lef' me, I gwine ride your tail until you regret the day you look on me at dat clinic; you follow? If you try use you cheap tactics and just slip away, you will know what that *Fatal Attraction* business was really 'bout. So yuh better sit you tail down and talk to me."

She said all this staring directly into his face, in a calm voice that made it all the more sinister. When she finished, Ferron slowly walked back to the bed and sat down.

"I don't know what is wrong with me," he said quietly.

"You don' respect me, tha's all," she said simply.

"That's not true . . ."

"No, no . . . I not saying you don' like me or that you don' love me; maybe you might; but you don' respect me. You put things to me that you wouldn' put with you Delores, she. No. You see, me, I am the one with the sugar daddy, right; the girl who give herself for a little support; a woman who can' even talk 'bout university or nothing like that. So you look on me, an' you say: 'I couldn' marry her. Where we would be in five years, ten years?' You know. So you look on that an' you say: Well, is a ting. A ting. Tha's all—a passing ting. A short-term ting. An' who know how short? An' Mitzie must know that sometimes a man will fuck a woman not out of love, not out of disrespect for his true love, but jus' because right then an' there, tha's what him need to make a moment complete. Mitzie would know that 'cause she do the same already an' she know, like any hard-survivor Jamaica woman know, that love is a ting that might jus' come an' go. Not so, Ferron? Oh yeah, 'cause my kind of loving is different from uptown loving, nuh true? Well, you gwine learn another ting, okay? Jus' don' come with you 'I am not good enough for you' shit! Everybody know that, so I giving you the best what I have. Tha's all. Bwai, grow up, man, grow up."

They sat in silence. Mitzie got up and turned on the radio. A regular radio drama series—people discussing the scandals and intrigues of a small urban community, a village tucked into the belly of the city. The room was quite dark now, and they could smell fish frying next door. A sound system rumbled into action some distance away. Ferron's mind was quite blank. Mitzie had read him, outplayed him, and taken him away from his plan. She was right. It was useless admitting it. She did not expect him to. She did not want him to admit anything. He felt the relief he had hoped for, nonetheless. That she read him so well, spoke out his doubts, called him on everything, allowed him to relax. She knew it all and wasn't tossing him out. He wanted to stay around her all night. The silence did not bother him. He just wanted to be around her.

"I didn't cook nothing tonight," she said casually.

"We could go get something," he offered.

"Like what so?"

"Fish. Fried fish," he said.

"You smell it too, eh?"

"Smells damn good." He felt even more relaxed.

"Come, mek we go beg them some." She was already tying her head.

"You sure? It is their supper . . ."

"What wrong with you, Ferron? You ever see Ma Elsie cook for she one yet? Anyway, she minding the baby tonight so you can see her. I will just give her a smalls for a plate, you know?"

Ferron stood in front of her as she moved to the window. "What is her name?" he asked.

"What you mean what she name? She name Elsie . . ."

"No, no, the baby."

Mitzie paused for a few seconds, looking at Ferron carefully with a hint of caution and disapproval. Then, as she pushed her feet into her slippers, she spoke somewhat under her breath. "Den nuh Sharon she name?" she said, as if it was the most obvious thing in the world and she was dealing with a very stupid child.

"I never know that, you have never told me her name."

"Well, it's Sharon," Mitzie said with finality.

"Thank you."

She moved to the window and shouted, "Maa Elsie! Fix two plate, nuh?"

Elsie's voice floated back in that high-pitched tone: "Yuh tink is restaurant I running, girl?"

"Come," Mitzie said, walking to the door.

"Okay . . . You is something else." Ferron stood up, laughing.

"You think?" Mitzie said, moving toward him. She embraced him and kissed him.

"Yeah, yeah," he said.

"Ferron, listen to me. Me not looking nothing from

you, you understand? I not looking for you to mind my pickney. I not looking for you to mind me. I can mind myself. I not looking no hero. I just like you. And you like me. You can manage dat?"

"Yeah, yeah man . . ."

She held his face between her palms. "Yuh sure?"

"Yes man . . ." he said with complete sincerity.

"Well, don' feel this done, dog," she said firmly. "No, no. Yuh hurt me; you better understand dat. An' I don' like a man hurt me. Next week we going somewhere, me and you, to talk, to work out your foolishness; to work out this business with you and your father. Simple."

"We are?" He was smiling.

"I not joking, you hear?" she said. "Serious business. If you don' pick the place, I will pick it. If you love me, Ferron, don' fuck wid this."

She kissed him quickly and then walked out the door. Ferron followed. It was pitch black outside. He kept close to Mitzie. She knew her way in the dark.

Unpublished notes of George Ferron Morgan

Who, I wonder, invented the principle of red chairs in this office? There are eight red chairs, indicating that their occupiers have a "higher" standing, are heads of departments. They are the deputy editor, Star editor, assistant editor, news editor, features editor, supplements editor, office manager, and that horrible (obviously Gardens) girl who heads a department of two called "Action Station"—truly garrulous and vulgar. The use of these red chairs is the method of keeping the workers in their place, and it works. The red-chair occupiers are extremely arrogant (they even walk arrogantly) and those chairs are sacrosanct. No one who is not designated as an occupier would dare, under any circumstances, even to "cotch" his or her backside on a red chair. But the hierarchy is breaking down. I notice that only the office manager stands up when the editor approaches. Democracy is creeping in, but the red chairs are sacrosanct.

I suppose that I am not impressive in this office. I came in, was slipped in dubiously, and I have made no real effort to be nice to people. The resentment is deep. The editor's secretary tries to treat me like dirt, the way she treats everybody, but I ignore her, even the sad death of her three-year-old daughter. (I think too much was made of it, anyway.) She has all the earmarks of a graduate of the Gardens. At least once a week she manages to gather a group of gawking onlookers around her to hear a harrowing report of some brutal murder just outside her area. She offers details with the relish of a man telling a deeply pornographic tale. Then she sighs and mutters something to the effect that, "Thank God those things don't happen in my area."

But everyone knows that she is talking about the people in her area who protect the area and how brutally they do so. Death, for her, is ordinary. I imagine her to be capable of anything. This is the price of our politics.

The other secretary is probably worse because she is lacking in intelligence; she has a very vicious eye and does not speak English under any circumstances. The third secretary has a pleasant personality and seems to be skilled in the ways of the office, but I get the impression that she has been passed over or kept down. The editor is playing a three-card trick between them.

They know how pathetic I am. They feel no pity for me. They know I belong to the other party and my presence here is a reminder that they won. I sense that there is a part of them that would like to stone me or lynch me right here in this press room. It is all so absurd, the lines that are drawn. After all, they know nothing about me. It may be my fault. I say nothing to them. I sit here, stoic, quiet, and to them, I must seem like a condescending bastard. I represent everything they loathe. I have a job because the editor is my friend. Me, the enemy, manages to get a job because of connections. And I am probably earning more than all of them, they think. They don't know that I agreed to pocket change, because I would agree to anything that would allow me to feel productive in some way.

If I fell flat on my face right now, a quick heart attack or something, they would saunter over, look down at me, then move to the window frowning, spit, and then call for the janitorial staff to come and deal with the mess. I swear, though, I would crawl to one of those red chairs and expire all over it.

SEVENTEEN

Theresa called at four o'clock in the morning. The phone rang twelve times. Ferron answered.

"Ferron . . ." She was crying. "Is your mother there?"

"She is sleeping." Ferron was looking through the window to see if the other houses had power. Power in their house went earlier that evening. Clarice went out, his mother went to bed, and Ferron stared into the darkness until he fell asleep on the sofa.

"Oh, sorry . . ." Theresa was whispering.

Ferron liked Theresa for her ability to love Femi. It took a certain daring to love a man whose presence was never guaranteed. She called Femi for all her significant decisions. Whenever Femi arrived, Theresa was his. Once, she had thrown a young man out of her house for Femi's sake.

"Okay . . ." Ferron wanted to wash his mouth. It tasted sour.

"I am looking for Femi . . . Have you seen him? Is he there?" She sounded worried.

"No," Ferron said.

"Ferron, I think he is screwing around with me. I mean with somebody else. He is, isn't he?" There was something almost accusatory about the question. Ferron felt the need to defend himself by disassociating himself from Femi.

"I don't know . . . Haven't seen him in a while. But you know Femi," he said slowly. Then he realized he could be honest by simply quoting Femi. "As he says, when he is in Jamaica you have all his attention."

"Yeah, right. I know the bitch!" she said sharply, then fell silent.

Ferron wanted to tell her that she did know Femi, that she knew that Femi had other links in Jamaica that he had to give time to. Those women, like Theresa, were not demanding, they understood that they each owned a certain part of Femi, a part that he gave fully with sweat, tears, and sperm. But it was all they got, and they had to understand that there were others who got the same. Ferron wanted to say this but did not. It was not something he had ever said to Theresa. This kind of openness from Theresa was unusual. She rarely spoke to him about Femi or about anything intimate. Quite some time ago he thought she'd been interested in him. She'd virtually said as much. Nothing came of it because he felt embarrassed and uncertain. She did not press. In retrospect, he decided that his timidity cost him a sexual encounter with an older woman. But the dream—the possibility— served a useful role as a disposable fantasy to accompany masturbation. So things reverted to normal. He started to notice the thin lines around her gray eyes, the sag of her breasts, and the cigarette stains on her fingers. He noticed that she had no bottom, that her cheekbones were too sharp and awkward on her face, and that her skin was leathery. He noticed the way her hands trembled before she smoked a cigarette, and her insistence on wearing dashikis and African cloth to every function she could attend. He noticed that she always wore makeup now. Always. He noticed her self-mocking attempts at dreadlocks with thin hair that was graying quickly. Black as he was, he knew he would not be black enough for Theresa. Theresa worked hard at eking out the black in her. It showed in her skin: leathery and worn with too much sun, as if she were daring the skin to defy the black blood in her system and break out in insidious skin cancer. Theresa was his mother's friend.

"I know it, though. He *is* fucking around." She started to cry again. "I . . . we just had a disagreement . . ."

"Theresa, I don't know where he is. I mean . . ." Ferron stopped. He felt awkward. Theresa was sobbing loudly on the phone and he did not know what to do, what to say. He wanted to hang up.

"I am sorry, Ferron," she said. She laughed a little and he decided that she was drunk. "I just feel badly, you know? I've been waiting a long time now and, well, I was getting kinda worried, with him and this business with your father. I thought maybe you might know . . ."

"No . . ." Ferron had last seen Femi a week ago at the Institute. Femi was there on business, trying to arrange for a group of Nigerian master drummers to come to Jamaica for a series of workshops. He had said that things were getting more and more interesting on the "espionage front." He said this with a wink. That was all. Then he left.

"Well, sorry to wake you up," she said. "Oh, Ferron, you people have power?"

"No. Went out at around eight," Ferron said. "You?"

"Same here. I feel like a dog, eh? I was just worried. So when you moving out?"

"I've moved out already. Just here to help Mother. She's moving tomorrow."

Theresa seemed to have recovered. Ferron relaxed. "Such a shame, eh? Was a damned nice place," she said. "But things change like that all the time."

"Yes," Ferron said. He looked outside. His eyes were getting used to the absence of light. The road was empty except for two dogs coupling angrily in the road. The bitch pulled away quickly and jumped over a fence into her yard. The other dog trotted to the fence and watched. Hungry. Ferron chuckled.

"It's just that the bitch is a little girl, you know? We get insecure sometimes, we old women," Theresa said. She laughed a light, faraway laugh. It stirred something in Ferron. "We are always holding on desperately. It's not love. Don't be fooled."

There was a long pause. Ferron wanted to say that he was not fooled, that he sometimes used to feel that Theresa wore her sex like a perfume and exuded it wherever she went. He wanted to tell her that she could do whatever she wanted, because she had the power in the careless way she spread her legs when she sat down, because of the vulnerability in her tiny bones and thinning hair. He wanted to tell her he had dreamed of her many times, a small woman bouncing against his body angrily, loudly, pulling at everything in him. Just there, suddenly like that, he had shifted from indifference to blatant lust. It was happening a lot these days. He could not predict when it would happen, or with whom. It just happened. And when it did, it all made sense. Like it made sense now, staring out into the stark street, the darkness distancing him from his own body, bringing Theresa closer, as if beside him, timeless and without context. Maybe it was the dogs. But he did not speak.

"I hope I am not keeping you up," she said. "From something else you would rather be doing."

"No. No. I was just dozing off. It is quiet. I was just dozing, I don't mind talking," he said.

"You know, there is a boy next door who spies on me. A schoolboy, really. For almost a year now, this one been looking over, eh. He will turn off his light anytime I come into the room, and wait. And every time I'm about to dress, I close the blinds. I used to find it funny. Kind of ridiculous, even a bit annoying." She was laughing softly. "Then today, I didn't shut the blinds. I let him watch, and I know he was watching, but it wasn't funny anymore. I felt flattered. Frightening, eh? Shit. I think I getting old. It bothers me. I might do something desperate, you know?"

"Like what?" he said, walking into her trap. And she spoke as if her throat were sore, as if her face were clouded with heat, as if her words were deep secrets only for him.

They talked till the road turned orange with morning.

Unpublished notes of George Ferron Morgan

There was an atmosphere during the war, during my school days at
Jamaica College, of an absolutely aristocratic dispensation. It is difficult to explain, now, that I went to a white school, which had some
rich blacks and scholarship boys. There were middle-class blacks
who could not afford to be boarders and were day boys. We (including the black scholarship boys) despised them. Being a boarder at Jamaica College set you in the highest possible class. I remember how
quickly we tried to show the poor boys (whom we called "toes") that
we were no longer part of them. I was made captain of third eleven
cricket and we were to play a match against boys from the Half Way
Tree school. This was part of Reg Murray's social work. The boys
("toes") arrived from Half Way Tree and sidled in by the bottom gate.
We sat under the divi-divi trees and ignored them. It was not yet time
for the match.

Suddenly an irate Reg Murray burst from his study. "Who is the
captain of the third eleven team?"

"I am, sir," I said, getting up.

"The team from the Half Way Tree elementary school have arrived. You must go and meet them. They are your guests."

I went to greet them, very shaken. They thrashed us that day. It
is an aristocratic trait that you are very courteous and generous to
your inferiors. The point is that I had been to an elementary school
exactly like the Half Way Tree school. Another thing that one found
was that most of the black boys (including scholarship winners)
had attended private preparatory schools and not public elementary

schools. One had to hold on to the thing that singled one out. In my case it was Africa, although they despised Africa in general. Africa meant that you had traveled through England and it was likely that your father had gathered up gold in Africa. I remember pointing out to my friend Ramsay Tull that I spoke with an English accent when I first arrived in Jamaica (which I did). Quick as a flash he said that I probably spoke with a cockney accent (which I didn't), but the point was made—an English accent, in spite of the barbarity of Africa.

Our family, though, was very much in that kind of privileged middle class. Our eldest sister was a boarder at St. Andrew High School, my brother was a boarder at Calabar High School, and the younger sister won a scholarship to Wolmer's Girls. My father bought a Ford Model T when he returned from Africa in 1930 and changed it for a Ford V8 in 1934 and then, with the war, we had an Anglia which was used almost exclusively (apart from taking me to and from school) by my brother. My father had two houses in Kingston, two houses in Sturge Town, and a hundred acres of land (Catherine Warren) just outside Sturge Town. By the sixties it had all gone. I am not aware that we made any great showing, any attempt to outdo our neighbors, but certainly my big sister had style, and before the sixties, that is for thirty years, we never seemed to want.

It's all gone. Were I to go now, I would be leaving debt. So much for the continuation of generational wealth. I like to joke that I am a socialist, and so I must not own anything. It almost sounds Christian. I was stupid, of course. I have left these children nothing. My brother consumed all that my parents left, and now all I have is class and nothing else. All gone. Every bit of it.

EIGHTEEN

The sun battered Ferron's head. He was sweating. He could smell the heavy musk of his own armpits. He needed a shower. New Kingston was dozing in the two o'clock lull. He walked slowly. She would still be there. Anyway, he did not want to get there too early and have to wait in the lobby for her to finish. There was nothing to do in the dusty room except listen to the clanks and moans of the men grunting under their weights. He slowed near the Air Jamaica building to catch some shade under a row of sparsely leaved trees. That is when he saw Femi bouncing out of the building grinning. Ferron looked away but Femi had seen him. He walked over laughing, his dark glasses catching the glare of the sun. Femi wore his dashiki today, and a light-blue skullcap.

"Ahh. You have been avoiding me," he laughed. He reached his palm out and shook Ferron's hand firmly. Ferron winced.

"Been busy, man," Ferron said.

"Ah. Your mother tells me that you think I am causing too much trouble." Femi was rarely less than direct.

"My mother is mourning." Ferron tried to smile.

"So should we all. Mourning is good." Femi looked at his watch. "What are you doing now? We could get a drink, eh? I have a few minutes. I think I should keep you abreast of the developments."

"I have an appointment," Ferron said quickly.

"Ahhh." Femi looked disappointed.

"Traveling?" Ferron could not help asking.

"You haven't heard, eh? Trouble at home. Well, not really trouble, but things are moving, cooking, as they say. America says they want Democracy, eh? So we give them Democracy. Now we are legitimate. I think I will give up this diplomatic shit and go back into the trenches. I miss bullshitting my way into the hearts of people."

"Pretty cynical," Ferron muttered.

"I was never cut out for this shit, anyway. I belong with the people. You stay in these comforts too long, you lose touch, you know. Lose the edge." He cleaned his dark glasses on the dashiki. His eyes were red. Ferron could smell the brandy.

"Develop a paunch." Ferron tried to be manly about his banter. Femi seemed to demand it.

"Don't take this wrongly, but . . . Well, that is what happened to your father, you know. And God knows, I won't let it happen to me. You die like that . . . it is not right." He tried to catch Ferron's eye for some approval.

"He was happy," Ferron lied.

"He was the fucking saddest man on this earth, and you know it. Don't ever, ever lie to yourself about that. Don't do that," Femi said. Ferron saw his eyes filling. He managed to hold it back, but he went silent. "Never."

Ferron dropped his head downward; he did not want to embarrass Femi by looking in his eyes.

"I mean, I had the job almost ready, it was just a matter of . . ." he said slowly.

"Look, it is over." Ferron could feel his anger growing. He was not ready to confront Femi today. Not about that, not now. It would leave him empty, weak. He wanted to be in the right mood for Mitzie. She could read into his moods, and if he seemed preoccupied or uneasy, she would leap into him, as if relishing his vulnerability. She had grown more vicious since she found out that he had spied on her. All he wanted to do this evening was to kiss, to touch her, to feel her orgasm clinging to him. He had to be prepared. Femi was trying to get his attention.

"Anyway, I may have to go home soon." He looked at his watch again. "Can we give you a lift? Oh, come on, Ferron, let's get out of this bloody sun, man. Theresa is waiting."

Ferron hesitated, then thought of seeing Theresa. He was tempted to see her reaction. They walked to the back of the building where Theresa was sitting in a black BMW. It was not her car, Ferron was sure of that. But she had managed to get a car for Femi. This one, he was certain, had a working air-conditioning system. She was sitting in the front seat reading the *Gleaner*. Ferron tried to stay calm. He sat in the backseat. She turned and smiled at him. Femi toyed with the knobs on the radio.

"We have to finish this thing before I leave. This investigation. They are dragging their feet. Look, Ferron, I would talk to your brother about this, but he is too buried in this church nonsense to even begin to understand."

"You would be surprised," Ferron said, "how in touch he is with what is happening." He was looking at the naked nape of Theresa's neck. It was slightly red, where Femi had nibbled.

"You think I am making more of this, eh?"

"Not really." The air conditioner had kicked in. Ferron sat back. He could kill a few minutes and then he would have to leave. He wondered if Femi knew about them, the phone calls. For no good reason, he felt like Theresa's secret lover—the intimacy of the phone call, the talk of sex, his erection and the thin film of sperm in his underwear after they had finished talking. Theresa's coyness now, her unwillingness to make eye contact, assured him that she felt the same way. It was absurd. The woman was so much older than him, and yet, in his presence, she assumed a youth and seeming immaturity that was curious. "Not really," he repeated. He realized that he did not feel any regret for doing this to Femi. None whatsoever.

"Your father was a revolutionary, and revolutionaries never die by accident," Femi said, turning around. "You understand that?"

Theresa started the engine. Femi turned to face the front.

"Yuh hungry, Ferron? We going by Devon House," she said, peering at him through the rearview mirror. Their eyes made contact. She held his gaze for a while. They shared a secret.

"I have to meet somebody. At the gym," he said. He noticed a slight wince in her face. Her smile slowly retreated.

Femi was checking his tickets.

"When are you leaving, Femi?" Ferron asked.

"Don't know yet. Still have some time. I have a meeting with that woman, the minister . . . Vera Chen, I think her name is. We have to work out a plan of action, you know."

"He is fucking her, you know," Theresa said, laughing. Ferron wasn't sure how to react.

"You want that to happen, don't you?" Femi laughed. He was very calm about the whole thing. "She's a lesbian, you know that."

"Well, just don't pretend you can't remember her name, alright?" Theresa said sharply.

"I wish your imagination was reality," Femi said, turning to Theresa. "I would have already fucked the Queen of England."

"Maybe you have." Theresa stopped smiling. "Maybe you have fucked her and Lady Di and the fucking House of Windsor. Why leave them out?"

They were at a traffic light. Ferron quickly opened the door and stepped out. "Look, I will see you," he said.

Femi opened his door quickly and shouted over the roof: "I am telling you, Ferron, they killed him! I am not making it up!"

"I believe you," Ferron said, walking toward the sidewalk.

"Then why the hell are you avoiding me?" Femi seemed genuinely concerned.

"I've been busy. It's just been hard, Femi. Look, I will call you, alright."

"Ferron, he was your father!" Femi shouted.

"That's right, Femi. My father. So they killed him; what am I supposed to do with that? What are you going to do with that? You have someone to kill? This is not a damned Shakespearean play, Femi. I did all that I had to do. You do what you have to do, but just bear in mind that our histories with him are different, eh?" He could see that Femi wanted desperately to talk. But the traffic was picking up behind them.

"Move the rass car, man. You think this is yuh living room?" a man yelled as he weaved past them on his bike.

"I will call you, man," Ferron lied.

"Make sure you do that." Femi sat back in the car and slammed the door shut. Theresa was wiping her face. She did not look at Ferron. They drove off.

Ferron was not sure if she would call him that night as she had promised. He walked toward the black-walled, zinc-roofed building that stood on an intersection just outside of New Kingston. She would be finished now. Showering, perhaps. He hoped that the air conditioner would be on in the lobby.

Unpublished notes of George Ferron Morgan

Music was one of my father's things. We had always had a piano and my brother was a trained musician and so was my sister. I wasn't trained at all but taught myself to read music and played what I could of Beethoven and Chopin and some of the others. But I learned to play jazz by watching my brother. At a certain time (I must have been in sixth form) I took to composing, actually writing down the notes and chords with great precision. It was weird. I wanted to get out of the sixteen-bar round. My brother looked at these pieces and said (very hurriedly, I thought) that he couldn't read them. I hope he meant that they were unreadable. They have disappeared. But I became the jazz pianist at school in my last two years and enjoyed it no end. (I even played behind T.P. Bates's mouth organ at Oxford in 1949.) In those days parties were piano-parties and one became known as a pianist and one was always in the team that played. My own shyness prevented me from ever really learning to dance in an orthodox way. Foxtrots, one-steps, waltzes, tangos, etc., never entered my repertoire. I have (after Oxford and with the help of liquor) managed calypso and African highlife, nothing more. What I became, up to the seventies, was an aficionado of jazz, particularly what used to be called bop or progressive. Affluence in Africa gave me the chance to buy records, but since returning to Jamaica my interest has been flagging, especially as jazz is removed from public entertainment on television and radio and I do not have a radio powerful enough to get the BBC. My son Ferron does, but he doesn't listen to jazz.

NINETEEN

Ferron found himself playing games when he talked to Mitzie, and she understood the games and joined him. They met in Hope Gardens in the evenings and once she brought the baby with her. It was a girl and suddenly Ferron decided that this was his child. He asked about the baby a lot and thought of a time when they would talk to each other—the baby and himself. Mitzie was amused, nothing else. She didn't encourage him.

They played games with words, especially when it came to very intimate things, things to do with sexuality. One evening the sun was sinking and they decided to stay longer in the gardens and climb the fence after. They sat there silently looking out and then, for no apparent reason, she began to tell him about her first time. She spoke slowly, as if trying to enter a world that she had stayed away from for years. She spoke as if she were savoring each word on her tongue, feeling the texture of the landscape of red soil, the bauxite smell in her nose, the green landscape of sloping hills. Ferron listened without interrupting. He was drawn into her world and he wanted to stay there, hidden.

"One day, I was home. I use to live with my father. My mother never stay with us. She was living with a nex' man. Well, one day, Daddy leave me alone in the house.

He said he was gwine come back late. When it get dark I hear somebody knock on the door. It was Mr. Jones. Mr. Jones was Daddy good friend; them use to work same place. Mr. Jones use to live in the same district so I use to see him. He was a nice man. I use to like him a lot because of the way he could tell jokes. I like people who can tell jokes good. Well, I tol' him that Daddy wasn' there but he said is not Daddy he come to look for and that what he wanted was to talk to me. Well, that man could talk and he make me so laugh that night that it just happen. He never raped me, even though I never want it at all, but after a little I couldn' help it, I was laughing. Tha's all I remember. Laughing, and then, after he left, crying. I jus' sit down and cry and cry. I know he was frighten and every time he see me after that he would ask me if I was alright. I never tell Daddy. I just stop go church and Daddy never ask no question. Well, everything was normal until it come back to me how Mr. Jones in the bar talking 'bout what a sweet lickle juicy girl I was and how Daddy don' know how to mind his own pickney. Das when I start hate him. It reach Daddy, but 'im neva say anything to me, but 'im stop talk to Mr. Jones. You see after that, when time I use to see that lickle monkey, I would spit mek him see. I never even go to his funeral. I hate the man. But I learn from him. That is man all the way. You see, if it wasn' for him, I would be in the church still, maybe have a good husband with good education like you, and happy. Mos' men, is only something them looking. That is why I like you: you is a nice guy, you not into them things."

She would say things like that, laughing at Ferron, almost teasing him, and he knew it. While she spoke, she rubbed her hand up and down his back as if daring him to remain unmoved by her presence. He wasr't, but he did not show it overtly; he just played word games that made her understand.

"You know too much, you know?" she said, pulling on his chin so that he would look at her. "I don't trus' people who know so much 'bout me. They use it."

"Who would I tell?" Ferron asked.

"Me," she said.

"What you mean?"

"Fling it right back in my face . . . That is how people stay," she said, staring hard at him. "You wouldn' do that?"

"No," he said.

"Promise?"

"Yeah man."

"Me serious, you know?" she said, still staring at him.

"I know, I know," he responded, avoiding her eyes.

"Good," she said, now smiling. Then she drew closer to him and spoke softly: "Now is your turn. You are not a virgin?"

It was a game. He was never explicit about what he wanted to say but he still wanted her to understand what he was getting at. She played the game even more deftly than he thought at first. His ploy was to get her to take the initiative, to be the first to suggest that they kiss, that they hold hands, that they touch. He wanted to respond, to be led. She understood this and allowed him the luxury he wanted—the freedom from responsibility. She knew exactly what he wanted, and she gave it to him in that teasing way. She did not mind the control, and she exerted it at times, really to make him uncomfortable, uncertain. Their game was a well-orchestrated pattern of hints, suggestions, half-statements, that begged for completion. The ground rule was simple: who could hold out the longest—who could say the most without committing, who could say the most with the least said.

"You love him?"

"Sort of."

"How you mean?"

"Well, 'im is a nice guy."

"How?"

"You know."

"No, I don't."

"'Im is gentle."

"You mean he doesn't beat you?"

"No sah. Yuh crazy?"

"How then?"

"How then what?"

"How is he gentle, then?"

"You know."

"I don't."

"We make sweet passionate love, love. Passionate like fire."

"Jesus Christ."

"You like that, eh? You like when I talk stoosh like that?"

"What?"

"The way I say that?"

"I just like to hear you talk. That is all."

Her eyes would sparkle with the game, daring, wanting to see him respond to her by being uncomfortable, uneasy.

"Maybe."

"You just trying to find my weakness, right?"

"What weakness?"

Eventually the words became flesh.

They kissed to see if they both agreed on what a good kiss was. It always began with the tongue, with words, then the tongues would come alive, fencing in the wet softness of their mouths. At nights, afterward, Ferron would feel a soreness in the thin membrane beneath his tongue.

Those were simple days. He woke in the mornings with just about enough time to take a shower and catch a bus to the university. He would work in the library all day, ignoring everyone around him. At lunchtime he bought a bag of water crackers and two bottles of soda which he would eat slowly and lazily under a huge guinep tree near the Student Union building. At the end of the day, he walked toward the gardens to wait for Mitzie. Usually she came a few minutes after he arrived. She was not working, but she seemed to have some appointment every day, just before they met. Ferron suspected that she was still seeing her "sugar daddy," but he did not mention it—he was afraid to bring it up; afraid of what he would hear, afraid of what she would do, what she would demand of him. They would stay in the park until about nine o'clock, then they climbed the gate to get out since the park closed at about six o'clock. They would walk to the bus stop and take the bus down to Half Way Tree where they usually parted ways. She headed for the Maxfield Avenue bus across from the broadcasting station; he would linger in Half Way Tree Square until the last bus to his home was loading up. He would head home, go directly to bed, too tired to think, too tired to open his mail. He lived in a hole during those weeks and the only person who saw him alive was Mitzie. Theresa called almost every night at about two o'clock in the morning. He listened to her share intimacies, her longings, her feelings for Femi. He offered little of himself, but she never seemed to mind. The talk became very sexual sometimes, and she would tease him, ask him what he was doing. One night she thanked him for a great call when they were saying goodbye.

"Did you notice?" she asked.

"What?" He was dying to get into bed and sleep.

"My breathing. Did you notice my breathing?" She laughed.

"What about it?"

"Oh, nothing. Forget it. I just wanted to thank you. You help me a lot . . ."

"Okay," he said. He must have sounded a little impatient or uncertain, because she spoke quickly, giggling.

"You're sounding nervous. Don't worry about it. We're like that, we women. I just wanted to thank you, not freak you out, alright?"

"I see," he said. Unsure of where to go with this.

"You think I am crazy, right?" There was a certain anxiety in her voice. "You don't think I should have done it."

They talked on for an hour after that.

Unpublished notes of George Ferron Morgan

How on earth did I develop an interest in politics? My father was not a politician that one could see, but he did bring Booker T. Washington and Aggrey to my attention and I believe that he took me to hear Marcus Garvey—or, to put it correctly, I was with him on one occasion when he went to listen to Marcus Garvey. He never made a thing of it.

Sixth form must have been the time, but I came to politics through literature. A number of factors must have been around in sixth form. Shelley, Public Opinion, the school magazine, and poetry. What I remember is the story about Roy Ashman's essay, based on Joad's "Why War," which ended with the words, "I am a communist because I am an atheist and a coward." This was in a school magazine and created a scandal on the verandas of upper St. Andrew where they still sat discussing scandal when Roy Ashman's Spitfire ran into a mountain over Spain. Perhaps I wanted to emulate that fine spirit who had been kind to me (he was a very good jazz pianist and he encouraged me).

TWENTY

The next day, Ferron took a minivan down to Half Way Tree to catch a bus to Norbrook. Half Way Tree was sweltering in the midday haze; a dead dog stunk in a garbage heap behind the bus stops. The Norbrook van was empty, the only bus at the stop. He hoped another van would come along. This would whip the men into action and precipitate a veritable race all the way to Constant Spring. Everything was predicated on the principles of competition. At the moment there was no competition, so the driver and conductor were taking a break. The driver sat on the crumbling wall that overlooked a gully littered with debris from decades of storm run-off and indiscriminate dumping. The driver sipped a cold Red Stripe, watching out for another bus to come careering around the corner.

Ferron hoped Uncle Wayne would know where the key was. He had never been unwilling to let Ferron have the place, but he relished the ritual of being asked. What was disturbing was the danger that one day he would simply forget that he owned this cottage, that he did have keys, that he did have relatives. Ferron feared that one day he would visit him and the old man would look blankly at him, not recognizing him. It would be fitting retribution. The truth was that none of his relatives visited him for anything other than to get something from him: information, the keys, old papers, and so on. Beyond that, Uncle Wayne was dead. He had declared this himself several years ago. *I am no longer a living member of this family. My will is completed. If you have not heard from my lawyers, that should tell you something.* This was how his open letter to the family ended. No one spoke about it, perhaps out of deference to Old Man Ferron, who, it was felt, had suffered so much at his brother's hands that to speak of this would have been insensitive. Uncle Wayne was dead.

His declaration had come when he moved to the retirement home in Norbrook. The former mansion of some well-to-dos who abandoned the country in the early seventies, this well-manicured home was the destination of the wealthy and well-situated. It was staffed by a team of efficient and uniformed women who had learned to serve these people in a manner that reminded them of another time. They were well paid to take all kinds of crap and nonsense with a professionalism that always impressed Ferron when he visited. He was struck by their pragmatism: never angry, never mumbling, never fawning or overly friendly, just efficiently playing the roles of "maids" these people expected.

Uncle Wayne was detached from the present as well as the family. He surrounded himself with things that reminded him of some forty or fifty years ago: photographs, paintings, magazines, books, furnishings—just about everything he kept in his room. The irony of what he was attempting was not lost on him, but he was quite clear about how he wanted his world to look. While he recognized visitors, he rarely welcomed them. Those he really did not care to see were treated with absolute blankness. He was not beyond pretending a kind of Alzheimer's when he wanted to get rid of people. At least it was never personal, always democratic. Ferron had watched visitors—an old lover or some lawyer acquaintance—left to feel quite foolish standing there. They would leave in embarrassment.

With Ferron, he seemed to make an exception—as if his nephew was his one reminder of a life beyond the home. He would talk about the past, but more often than not he would make silly, disparaging jokes about the poor education that Ferron must be getting at university, about the dullness of young people today, and repeatedly he would speak of the "poverty" of Ferron's father—his idiotic Marxism and generosity that could only wreck his life. When Uncle Wayne heard about the old man's death, he laughed: "I have been dead for how long? Four years, five? And nobody's buried me yet. Now look at him, dead for a few days and already he is buried . . ."

"We cremated him," Ferron said.

"Bad idea, bad idea," he muttered. "Not good for the ozone, you know? Did they burn him naked or clothed?"

"I don't know," Ferron said. "We did not get his clothes back. But I never went to ask for them."

"I would prefer to be burned naked. But I prefer burial," Uncle Wayne said, staring into the trees. "Sometimes I lie down here with my eyes closed, and I try to move my limbs, and I can't. I feel as if my brain is working, but the rest of me isn't. I can't even hear my heart. I feel very dead. I know that if someone were to come in and check me, you know, look at me, they would think I was dead. Imagine someone burning me in that state. It must be painful as hell." He stopped and laughed at his

accidental joke, then repeated the words slowly: "Painful as hell."

He, like everyone else, had expected that he would
die before his younger brother. It was not so much his
age—although he was in his late seventies—but his body,
its will to go on. Ravaged by years of alcoholism, wretch-
ed and violent marriages (he was always the abused
one), cigarette-smoking, Uncle Wayne had suffered two
major heart attacks, a stroke, and at least four death vig-
ils (one after a tragic car accident when a close friend
died—they were both completely drunk). They waited,
he waited. Death would not come. He would find his ap-
petite again, ask about the news, talk about the weather,
and then it would be clear to all that dead as his body
may have been, he was going to live on.

Had he continued to live in the run-down apartment on Molynes Road, a cubbyhole he had moved into
with an old retired prostitute friend, where he prac-
tised street law, advising thugs about their rights, about
how to beat the law—all for a beer or two, some food,
anything—perhaps he would have been killed or simply died of starvation. But his sojourn on Molynes Road
was not enforced. He always had the option of finding
his way out of there. It just seemed, for a long time, too
much work. This lack of will to do better would probably have killed him had a former lover from way back
in his past (and one-time sponsor) not died. This woman no one in his family had met, but they knew of her
because of three famously caustic letters that she had
written, berating them for allowing as brilliant a mind as
Uncle Wayne's to go to waste. She had singled out Old
Man Ferron for his jealousy, his mediocrity, and his mis-

guided indulgence in Marxism. She had "discovered" Uncle Wayne while he was studying at Yale. He met her in the middle of his second year, at a time when he was most in need. He seduced her and convinced her that he needed her help. His father had written to him at the beginning of that year to say that he would not be able to support Wayne for the rest of his studies. He should return to Jamaica, work for a while, and then travel to England where the education would be less expensive. Wayne's benefactor, impressed by his wit, charm, and apparent brilliance, decided to sponsor him. He finished his studies, and stayed in the United States for several years, living with this woman. Even when she threw him out over some sordid business with one of her maids and he called her a white cow and returned to Jamaica, she never stopped supporting him; it was, according to Wayne, her way of punishing him for insulting her— letting him know that since she had made him, she owned him. He was too lazy to resist. He accepted her money when he needed it.

Her decision to leave money for him was predictable. Even in death, he would laugh, she still wanted to have her slave under control. She'd had her attorneys arrange for Wayne's move to the home. Everything was paid. His "inheritance" had one critical stipulation: he had to spend it entirely on himself and could not leave anything for any of his heirs. Wayne accepted this gladly. This was the moment of his death. He complied readily, abandoning the room, the prostitute, and his street clients without as much as a word of farewell. He had summoned Ferron to help him move his things. These were not the few possessions he had in the Molynes Road room, but his old furniture and books which he'd kept for years in a storage area downtown. They discovered a hurricane a few years before had damaged the building and much of the furniture had been ruined. The books were either completely mildewed or being devoured by termites. They abandoned most of that stuff in a dumpster outside the warehouse.

It was hard for Ferron's family to accept the news of Uncle Wayne's virtual death, though there were compensations. A good number of his other books had been stored in their house, abandoned there after he'd shacked up with them following one of his most damaging legal wrangles. They'd become a regular obstacle to the washroom, but every time someone threatened to toss them out, the reminder would come: "Uncle Wayne says he will come and get these books soon." When he announced his death, they could at least give up on the prospect of his return and the books were taken to the abandoned chicken coop in the backyard—Ferron's mother's experiment with "self-help" farming during the socialist seventies (a mongoose had killed most of the chickens and the rest were stolen by the neighbors). For a while, the coop had been a clubhouse for a short-lived neighborhood gang: the Seven Black Bottles. Squabbles, dwindling interest, and school eventually thwarted their efforts. The coop was again abandoned— the black bottles (Red Stripe bottles painted with cheap black powder paste) still gathering dust on a roughly constructed shelf—and converted into a storeroom for garden tools and other items that were truthfully junk, but had that peculiar quality of seeming to be worth something. Eventually, Uncle Wayne's books were housed in it—and ravaged by the elements and by roaches. Clarice and Ferron had explored the boxes. They found intriguing documents—legal briefs, curious memos to himself, long legal affidavits, news clippings, and letters of varying lengths and interest that confirmed what the old man had muttered about Uncle Wayne: that he had, single-handedly, and without remorse, completely devoured the once-substantial fortune of the Ferron family. The anger and resentment that his brothers and sisters felt toward him was not unwarranted.

The damage was impressive: at one stage the grandparents owned five houses in Kingston, all in fairly well-to-do suburban areas. They also owned three houses in the country—two in St. Ann and one in the foothills of the Blue Mountains. One of the St Ann houses was the family home where the children grew up and attended Teacher Ferron's school. It was a two-story building with a complex of verandas that their light-skinned grandmother had lined with a shock of greens—vines, potted plants, hibiscus bushes, creating a cool greenness—verandas that offered wonderful views toward the sea on one side, and into the hills on the other. The other house was even more expensive and attractive. It was built a little lower down the hill on a small plateau. It was a bungalow with something like eight bedrooms and a detached house for the maids. Beside it was a sweet-water well, which was still used to supply water for washing although a more modern plumbing system had been put in place. There was a time, years ago, when his grandmother was alive, that Ferron remembered when myriad distant cousins and friends would come to the house for Christmas. People would fill up all the rooms and then spill out into the yard. There was no day or night. Time was spent eating, drinking, sleeping—in no particular order. His father drank a lot during those days, and then he would disappear into the hills with a bunch of the men—mainly laborers who revered the late Teacher Ferron—to carry out some rituals that brought him back days later with a weary look of purest satisfaction. This was soon after his return from abroad. With his reputation in the newspapers and his publications, the community saw him as Teacher Ferron returned. (Uncle Wayne was not highly regarded, and the sisters not held in much esteem since both had remained unmarried and childless.)

The Blue Mountain house was no more than a small cottage that had been the first of a series of similarly designed cottages built by a clever entrepreneur to create low-income retreats for middle-class Jamaicans. Wayne never sold the cottage but relied on a modest income from renting it out. Ferron had used the cottage for his personal retreats as well, and occasionally he arranged for friends of his—church and university friends—to retreat there. It would be ideal for Mitzie and him. There were no family memories locked up there; he wanted to stay far away from any such memories while with Mitzie.

All the Kingston houses had been sold by Uncle Wayne to pay off his debts. Ferron had only really thought about this after his father died and his only legacy was a debt of ten thousand dollars. They were leaving behind their well-furnished rented house. Ferron had taken for granted that the old man would leave nothing behind. He did not. But Uncle Wayne's years of plenty became a point of some resentment. As the only child then still at home in Jamaica, he'd had the task of managing their widowed mother's affairs. He sold everything he could to support a celebrity existence. A barrister of some fame, he would work when he felt like it and with whom he wanted. When the money was gone, he tried to take on more work, but became embroiled in an embezzlement scandal. The Bar came down hard on him and encouraged his suspension. It was the first of three suspensions before he was finally banned from practicing law in the mid-seventies. He started to drink heavily, still living off the money from the sales. By the time Ferron's father had returned to Jamaica to look after his mother, all the money was gone. Ferron's father had to take in his mother and his brother, both now virtually destitute. They fought a lot in those days about where the money had gone. Wayne was completely unrepentant. He had stayed; he had buried the old man; he had watched his blindness and death; he had comforted the mother, while the others were traveling. He deserved it all.

The country houses were not sold. Ferron could never understand why, and Uncle Wayne dismissed the question as silly. He liked the houses, and anyway, people were living there. He had ensured, however, that the homes were signed over to him, so he owned them. He rented one, the house on the hill, to people in the village, and the other was leased to the Jamaica Tourist Board. He got good money for these arrangements. No one was sure where the money went, or what he planned to do with the places when he died. But he was willing to let his nieces and nephews use the Blue Mountain cottage during the off-seasons. This was usually why Ferron saw him. This was why Ferron was taking the trip this time.

He and Mitzie would go through Mandeville, visit the scene of his father's passing, and then travel to the cottage. It was all he could manage now—a way out of the madness of these last few days.

Wayne sat in the backyard that spread in carefully undulating landscaping to a twelve-foot link fence. Beyond the fence was the Constant Spring Golf Course. The huge shade trees cooled the smooth cement patio on which deck chairs were placed every morning for breakfast. Uncle Wayne ate mangoes with a knife and spoon. It was an operation that he carried out with meticulous efficiency. When Ferron entered he had consumed one of five Bombay mangoes—squat green fruit with a sharp nipple at the end that looked like a bloated comma. He had the mangoes lined in a row.

Ferron sat down at the table, waiting for Uncle Wayne to acknowledge his presence. He looked something like his father might have looked in a few years had he lived. Uncle Wayne wore a lavender silk dressing gown over his pajamas.

His delicate fingers worked quickly, efficiently. His gray-brown eyes bulged slightly—a family trait that made the women look bold, alluring, as if their eyes were in constant dilation. His mouth moved quickly as he chewed the soft flesh. The tangy sweetness of the Bombay mango drifted into Ferron's nose.

First he selected a mango and weighed it in his right hand, as if trying to determine what attitude would shape his eating of this particular one. Then he put it on the saucer and picked up the sharp-bladed kitchen knife, which he wiped carefully with an already mango-stained napkin. Picking up the mango, he cut a circular line around its middle, slicing down to the seed. Tiny droplets of juice dripped onto the saucer. Placing the knife on the table, he held the mango at both ends and twisted it as if opening a bottle. A quick sucking sound and he had two pieces, one a hollow cup lined with glowing flesh, and the other holding the seed, which jutted out almost obscenely. Uncle Wayne cleaned his teaspoon with the napkin, and ate the cupped half, scooping lumps of flesh and slipping them into his mouth quickly. He scraped the inside of the cup until it became almost transparent, showing light through the green membrane. He picked up the second half, the grotesque piece. This time, he clutched the seed with his fingers and twisted it sharply until it plopped out of the skin, leaving behind a thick lining of mango. He lifted the seed delicately to his mouth and chewed and sucked on it until the seed was almost white in its nakedness. He then ate the final cup with the spoon—like a custard. Slowly this time. Burping softly, he placed the seed neatly in line with the others he'd eaten.

"Doctors say the skin is good for roughage, but I shit like clockwork."

Ferron stared at the spoils of his meal; in the bright light they looked like a carefully arranged still life, complete with the dappled shade and light from the overhanging trees—and that treacherous-looking knife. All that was missing from this picture was a carefully penned suicide note in sepia ink. This would complete a perfect symbol—grotesque, surreal—the bald white death of the seed: spent youth, a spilling of seed, fleshless after the *carne*-val of a wayward life.

"Always money, eh?" Uncle Wayne said.

"What?"

"Even when yuh dead, money determines your damn fate. Bury my ass, yuh hear? Bury every part of me. I want to reach heaven with my cock still attached, damn you." He laughed at his joke. "Anyway, who the hell want an eighty-year-old anything these days. They could buy them things in India cheap-cheap—young parts, you know? He gave his parts?"

"I don't know," Ferron lied. The old man's body *had* been ravaged for useful parts before the cremation. He would have wanted it that way.

"Well, bury my rass, you hear?" He began the third mango.

Ferron hesitated. He was waiting for a good moment to ask for the keys. Uncle Wayne knew why he was there; this ritual was just his way of making Ferron squirm—his bout of morning entertainment.

"So, you inherited big house and land, eh?" He chuckled.

"You know . . ." Ferron began. Then he saw the grin and felt foolish. "Yes, six houses, over a hundred acres of good land in St. Ann, a couple of cars, but we still fighting over the jet—that sister of mine is so damned greedy . . ."

"Not a damned thing, eh?" Wayne said.

"You know how it go." Ferron shrugged.

"I told you about socialists. Not a damned thing. Now you, you're a Christian, right? Running around with all them American evangelist type, doing your tongues business and all that, yes? Well, good. You better off with that kind of thing, you hear? You ever see a poor American preacher yet? Now, a preacher have the whole thing right—none of this socialist business. Leave that to the damned Catholics who got the Vatican to feed them when they are hungry . . . Every jack one of us is going to dead sometime, anyway. And if nobody is going to take the trouble to look back at your sorry life and write a book about it or some shit like that, then all you have is the life you lived—not no damned legacy, just the actual life. You think your father enjoyed his life, eh? No, no. That man was waiting for the book to come out about him, waiting for some accolade, some crown. But what does he get?"

Ferron thought of Femi and his plans—the process of canonizing Old Man Ferron. This was the book, but reduced to a series of contrived articles; a narrative about a heroic death that was already beginning to seem absurd. Five years before, at the height of the intrigues of the seventies, the story would have had greater value—not so much that it would have been believed then, for it was believed now—but because nobody cared these days about radical heroes with a commitment to Africa and Blackness. Femi's mission would have interested Uncle Wayne, but he did not read the current papers; he only read old magazines.

Uncle Wayne had stopped talking. He was staring directly at Ferron. Ferron could not keep his eyes off the tiny black moles that lined the puffed bags under the mischievous gray-brown eyes. Wayne was waiting for Ferron to take the bait, to mount a defense of his father, but he simply smiled and nodded. He turned and looked out to the golf course instead. A sprinkler had started to spray arcs of rainbowed droplets on the green. Crows circled above the trees. Back here, the serenity suggested another time, another place altogether—far from the snap of gunshots at night, the uncertainty of the knock on the door, the indiscriminate machete slash, the flame of madness. It was a different country, a tourist cliché of hummingbirds, flowers, and fruit trees. Uncle Wayne had seen enough, smelled enough, swallowed enough reality for a lifetime. At night, the home became a veritable fortress, a tomb locked from the inside, where old people drifted between dream and death, floating to the melancholy wash of some old ska music scratching its way through the hallways from Uncle Wayne's ancient gramophone player. He'd asked Ferron to bury him to the sounds of anything by Don Drummond or the Wailers that was recorded before 1965.

Rituals of predictability. That was what Uncle Wayne desired. Death, of course, had its own rituals in the home. The dead would lie there for a few hours before one of the nurses would come in and clean them up, humming a hymn—always a hymn. The body would be removed at lunch—always the next lunch period after the death—nobody explained why, but it was done this way, always. A band of pink ribbon would be placed on the bedhead until someone else replaced the deceased. No one spoke of the dead. After all, that is what they were all waiting for.

One afternoon Ferron heard an old very dark man of some girth arguing with a doctor who wore a white coat over his shorts and flowery T-shirt: "I don't want you cut off that damned foot too. I lost one already, that was enough, and still I going die, right? What I want, you know what I want? I want to sit out there on my porch, right, just sit out there and look on them hummingbirds, look on them trees, and look into that blue sky, and then I can just dead, you know. I don't want no damn amputation, alright?"

"But you will," the doctor started.

"Dead," the old man said, smiling. "What you think we here for, eh? This is not no damn convalescent home, man."

The man died the next day. A pink ribbon was on his bed. Ferron had seen so much death since his father's death. Death—in a way he had never noticed before—now appeared before him, defining itself, demystifying itself.

Uncle Wayne's reaction to his brother's death was laughter and an intense amusement at the irony of it all. He could muster little else. Today he was less giddy about it, but he brought up the business of avoiding the old man's habits again. Ferron found himself feeling a bit irritated. It may have been the growing heat on his neck as the sun shifted.

"They say he was killed . . ." Ferron secretly hoped that this would throw Uncle Wayne.

"We are all killed, you know?" Wayne said, without even missing a beat. He was smiling. "When we die, most of us, somebody harbors murder in their hearts for us—somebody wishes us dead—even if not callously or vindictively. I believe that the moment someone can imagine a world without you, a livable world without you, you are in danger. They can wish these things into being. I may have killed him, you know. You too."

Ferron said nothing. Uncle Wayne was not going to weep or mourn. It made everything absurd—his excuses over his sleeping around, his emotional neediness, his trauma, his darkest depressions. Ferron began to have second thoughts about asking for the key. He'd go back to Mitzie and tell her that this trip was a bad idea. He would deal with his headaches.

"The keys to the cottage on my dresser," Uncle Wayne said. "That's what you come for, right?"

"Well . . ." Ferron began, but stopped.

"Take some beer and a woman, get piss-face drunk, sleep, get drunk, sleep, fuck, get it out of you damn system . . ." He was beginning to sound like Femi. "Hell, when my old man died I don't remember much. I was piss-faced at the funeral. Nobody cried like me, and it was because I was worrying about whether I could stand up at the graveside—all that time in the church I was worried about if I could stand up in the graveyard." He stopped talking and rested his palms on the table. The skin looked almost transparent and delicate in its vulnerable pinkness. "Not a damned soul there to hold your hand. Nobody."

Ferron shook Uncle Wayne's hand, went to the room, got the keys, and left the cool of the home. He walked slowly to Constant Spring, his mind full of Uncle Wayne eating the mangoes with such meticulous care, such concern for detail, like a man who planned to live forever. Ferron decided that he was confused. What he could not determine was what he was confused about. He slept on the ride from Constant Spring to Half Way Tree.

When he woke, the familiar sourness in his chest and throat made him gag. His stomach was churning. He was hungry, but too hungry now to eat. The pressure was already growing at the base of his stomach. He leaned forward and tried to force a belch. Suddenly the press of the bodies on him was stifling. The van swerved in close to the sidewalk to offload passengers, and the lurching motion made Ferron dizzy and weak. Cold sweat beaded his forehead. He pushed out of the van with the rest of the passengers and then felt himself wobbling. He held on to a lamppost and waited. A woman stared hard and questioningly at him. "You alright?" she said with more accusation and curiosity than concern. He nodded. He waited for the colors of clothing and the tilting sky, the quick flashes of moving vehicles and the din of voices and vehicles to settle. He tightened his body, willing his stomach to keep everything inside. The smell of Bombay mangoes came back to him, this time as a too-sweet cause of nausea. He walked gingerly across the dusty park to catch another bus that would take him up toward the hills.

Unpublished notes of George Ferron Morgan

I was reading some old letters I found on the veranda stuck away in my folders yesterday. I was trying to find the birth certificate. It is hard to believe how organized I have been in my life. It is easy to be organized when you think that the world is going to cooperate with you. An organized office or papers is a sign of optimism. You actually think that the things you have collected over the years—the letters, the manuscripts, the scrapbooks, the clippings, the old bills—are going to be useful in explaining who you are in the future. Everything is in layers—it is like an archeological excavation. On the surface of that veranda is the chaos of my current life. Nothing is in order, everything is in sloppy piles and most of it is covered with rat shit— papers have been eaten by roaches and spoiled by rainwater. The deeper I go, the greater the order. Near the certificate were these letters. In those days I was optimistic.

They said they needed the certificate for me to get that job teaching in Mandeville. I am not even sure why I am taking this job. But I am getting to think of myself as quite useless nowadays. Here in this job, I am too close to the politics, too close to the realization that I can't do a thing about it. I am in a prison—like a prisoner of war, sitting among my victors who are the captors. I am waiting for the trial and then inevitable execution. They look at me as if they know me to be a dead man walking around this place. It is quite depressing. Every day I am writing these editorials, pretending that what is happening is reasonable, as if the death of this dream is something that is practical now. These men are scoundrels, every single one of them.

I remember when they were nothings, illiterates running around Kingston with nothing useful in their heads, preening and showing off and making no sense. When they did not even care that we were on the verge of our own revolution. Now they run things. And these working-class people around me, they are a part of this tragic mess. They don't even know that they have been used, been sold a worthless bill of goods. I know that some of them were at the rallies, screaming with glee at that fat swarthy politician who was rolling his body on stage, sweating and shouting: "You want shoes? You want American apple? You want grapes? You can't get none of that right now, but when you vote for we, you can get shoes, good shoes, people!" He almost said amen. So maybe I need to be elsewhere. Perhaps being at that high school, teaching these children Shakespeare, will give me a chance to escape. That will be my "Island," my "Siberia" where the climate will be horrible, and maybe there I can write a book far from the madness of this place. If I stay here, I will die. I know this. Maybe someone will shoot me, or maybe . . . I will die. I am nothing now.

TWENTY-ONE

Holding hands.

For Ferron it seemed the right thing to do. He kept looking straight ahead, very aware that Mitzie was peering at him. She was playing to the gallery, giving the people on the bus a sample of the lovers' game. He knew her eyes had that amused brightness. He tickled her palm and felt her smile grow into a small laugh, warm on the side of his face. She sat back, pulling him back with her, and started to play with his fingers, resting his hand on her lap. Her lap was warm.

Outside, trees rushed past. The air was growing thinner and cooler as they climbed higher into the hills. It had rained the night before and the mountainsides were scarred with dark-brown holes where boulders, which now lay broken and splintered on the road, had been dislodged. It was still slightly overcast. The wheels of the bus whistled against the wet asphalt.

Ferron felt growing nausea. The swerving roads had a lot to do with this queasiness, but he was still also somewhat upset with Mitzie and her overacting. She was being too playful, relishing the apparent embarrassment that Ferron felt when she played this absurd lovers' game.

The hills rose above them, soft against the steel-gray sky. The greens were lively, almost dazzling, and strangely overpowering. They literally overwhelmed any other colors on the landscape. Small red houses dotted the hillside like ladybugs crawling on a carpet of green fur. Small, vulnerable toys. Ferron could make out the cluster of red-roofed buildings of the military training camp. They would have to walk from there, farther up into the hills, toward a darker, cooler valley of intense greens and dense foliage. To get to the camp, they would take a shortcut, a hiking trail that was almost always muddy and difficult. From there, they would follow a small uneven asphalt track for about two miles before they got to the gate of the cottage grounds.

The people on the bus had warmed to Mitzie. They owed their presence on the bus to her. The minivan never went this far into the hills. They had already passed the junction where passengers were normally deposited to walk the rest of the way to where they were going. Mitzie had flirted with the driver, complaining about the pains she would feel in her legs after walking so many miles. She assured the driver that the road was not as bad as his conductor had suggested—and the people on the bus echoed her in a chorus. She told him that he was sure to have a few people to bring down from the top of the hill. He was flattered by the attention, by her apparent intimacy, by Ferron's embarrassment and silence. He grinned and drove on. The conductor hissed his teeth.

Ferron enjoyed the rush of air on his face. Tiny water droplets touched his skin and the cool on his face and body eased the nausea. He breathed in and belched softly.

"You alright?" Mitzie asked, her eyes warm on his face.

"Yes, man," he said, looking away. He squeezed her hand.

"You have sof' fingers." He did not respond. "You know? You know?" She squeezed the hands playfully.

"I know," he said.

She was counting them slowly, now. "You don' bite you nails?"

"No," he said. She pressed his hand on her thighs.

"I like your fingers," she said. He could feel her smiling again.

"Yes." His voice was distant.

"So you won' even look at me," she said. Then pulling on his chin, she made him face her. "You vex with me?"

"No," he said. Then he looked away.

He could feel the people on the bus watching them. It wasn't that they disapproved, but it just was not the kind of thing couples did on the bus. They could accept arms around each other or the girl resting her shoulder on the guy's chest, but the hand-holding thing was not normal, it was alien, belonging to foreigners or people trying to be foreigners. Ferron felt as if they were trying to size him up. He was sure that they were associating this kind of behavior with softness, the behavior of a man who was less than a man, even if reliable, faithful, and kind. It was not just the hand-holding—it was Mitzie's behavior and Ferron's lack of predictable reaction to it. Mitzie had presence. They had watched her take command and arrange the ride farther into the hills with the aggression, charm, and style of a consummate manipulator. She was clearly a woman who could make a big man sit down while she played games with his hands. Ferron did not have the energy to pull away his hand.

There was a skinny woman sitting in front of them on the other side of the bus. To Ferron she had the look of the woman by the morgue. Seeing her had disturbed him. It was the same ageless quality: neither old nor young, as far as Ferron could tell. She was just skinny and happy, completely immersed in herself, the kind of woman who obviously drank a lot of white rum and twirled her bony bottom around outside the bar with some huge-bellied, lustful man, too drunk to do anything about it. She was the kind of woman who was not ashamed to laugh loudly and shrilly in public, stamping her feet on the ground and pulling her skirt elaborately between her legs. She was the kind of woman who walked with a sway, legs apart, bottom jerking in an attempt to rotate, her head in the air, her sharp breasts jutting forward, and her arms swinging elaborately at her sides. This was the kind of woman that Ferron worked her out to be, and so far she was proving him right. She stared at them with her dazed red eyes, as if expecting something really scandalous to happen. She had a permanent grin on her face, one that seemed to say: *Go ahead, go ahead, I want to see.*

At first, Ferron was convinced that Mitzie had not noticed the woman staring. She kept doing what she was doing as if there was no one else on the bus. But she kept increasing the sensuality of her game. It became clear to Ferron that Mitzie was giving this old/young wizened woman a show.

"Is far we have lef'?" Mitzie asked loudly, even though she was talking to Ferron.

The old lady cackled. "Heh, them cyaan wait!"

"Not much farther," he said, trying to be discreet.

"We gwine have to walk far?" she asked, pressing closer.

"It's a easy walk. It might be a little muddy, but we could clean up when we get there." He laughed slightly. He knew that the woman was waiting for her cue to break out in another cackle.

"Where we going wash off?" Mitzie asked with an innocent look on her face.

"The river," Ferron replied, smiling.

"You too bad," Mitzie said, squeezing his hand.

"Eh? What did I say?" Ferron asked, looking as puzzled as he could.

"You too bad, man," Mitzie said softly. The woman was chuckling. Then Mitzie grimaced, biting her lower lip with a wicked twinkle in her eye, and squeezed hard on Ferron's hand. "You too bad . . ."

"Oh God, Mitzie, no!" he said too loudly.

The woman clapped her hands with tremendous pleasure. "Heh heh heh heh." Her laughter was like rum, white rum, rich and sparkling, with a grating pleasure behind it that burned everything around. Ferron wasn't sure whether it was because he smelled it on her breath, but it was the only thing that could describe the laugh. White rum. It was both sensual and abrasive at the same time. It was old—old and young, innocent and knowing, shocked and encouraging.

"Young people," she laughed, throwing her head back. The laughter faded into a chuckle and a repetition of the words, "Young people."

Mitzie was still squeezing with a vivacious smile on her face.

"You're hurting me," he whispered to her.

"You too bad," Mitzie said. "That's what you want nuh. Gwaan. You want to see me naked inna river nuh?" She spoke softly and into his ear. Her breath was warm. He chuckled.

"I didn't say that," he said, managing to wrest his hand away. She quickly slipped her arm through his.

"Alright, alright, I won't squeeze it again," she said, taking the hand. "But you sof', eeh?" She kissed the fingers.

"Eh-eh. Yes, Lord," laughed the woman. "What a love making dis dough, massa!"

Mitzie calmed down after that. She had given an excellent performance and had drawn Ferron into it. That was what she had wanted. He was not so angry with her anymore. Soon the bus grew calm. The woman, growing bored with their stillness, turned to look at the road. The conductor had fallen asleep in the doorway. Ferron wondered if he would die if he fell out, but since the bus was not moving very quickly, he decided that the man would live. He was a conductor, and they did not die so easily. They always lived when all the passengers were dead.

The woman was the first to come off. She warned them about behaving themselves and to watch those soldiers. Ferron took that as a blow directed at him. The soldiers were the real men. But then she added that they should make sweet love and enjoy the river. She winked at Ferron. They watched her walk down the hill, just as Ferron had imagined she would, except she moved with far more elasticity than he had expected. Gradually the bus emptied until they were the last. Finally, the driver stopped the van.

"See the path there," he said without pointing. Ferron paid the fare, which Mitzie had managed to beat down to virtually nothing. The driver must have agreed out of sheer frustration. He was probably tired of Mitzie even though he liked her style.

As the bus wobbled down the hill, they stood in the middle of the road and watched. Then Mitzie declared: "Lawd, 'im ugly, eeh?"

Ferron laughed, enjoying her viciousness. Then he let her walk ahead while he directed her from behind. This was the first time she was really depending on him and it changed the way they talked. She was afraid that it would get dark with them still on the path, but he was not worried about that, he knew the way very well. The confidence he had and her dependence on it was a good feeling. They kissed once on the way up. It was accidental, almost. She was warm, giving. He sensed that she was worried about more than the darkness; she was too quiet; no more jokes.

They left the parade square as the sun began sinking behind a cluster of hills. They walked along a narrow asphalt road which was scarred with potholes that sometimes stretched like canals across the road. Brown, thick water, like blood, caught the periodic glow of fading sunlight peeping behind leaves.

They walked apart.

Above them the mountainside rose sharply. It was thick with bushes and trees. Insects created a din in the silence. Apart from these, there was only the sound of their footsteps crunching on the stones, and their breathing, labored and even.

They were not talking.

Ferron looked up. He saw the cottage. From the porch that overlooked the road he would watch hikers crawl like ants on the black line of asphalt. Sometimes he would shout out to the hikers. He was never sure whether the people heard him or only saw him when they waved back—often with enthusiasm and energy.

He imagined what he would see if he were looking down at them: two solitary figures walking at a distance. From up there he could make out male and female and he could see colors. He couldn't make out faces and he would not be able to tell how far apart or close they were. But if they came closer, he would see their faces. They were stern and distant, as if they were not in each other's company. If he could get even closer, into the brain perhaps, he would see his own anger and why it was festering like that.

Mitzie had flirted with the "sarge" and some of the soldiers. It was almost as if she wanted to destroy the growing closeness that they had felt on their way up the trail. Ferron kept hearing her silly remarks ringing in his ears, like when she said to the sergeant (who was making a joke about what they were planning to do up there): "Him? Cho, 'im is jus' a lickle fren'. Is like my brother . . . Him wouldn' do a ting. Is a Christian, you know? A good one too." She was laughing and she did not stop laughing when the soldier suggested that perhaps he should come and make sure that sensible things happened up there. She thought it was funny. Ferron was angry. He had smiled, or maybe he actually laughed, but when she looked into his eyes, she saw the deadness. She was suddenly uncertain. He could tell this because her laugh faltered. She turned away from him.

They walked the two miles in silence. When they got to the gate of the grounds she sat down on a stone at the side of the road. He could barely see her face in the darkness. He wanted to tell her that they should continue, but she seemed determined to sit there until they'd had it out. He waited, standing some way off.

"You are not my man," she said angrily.

"I never said I was," he responded, almost to himself, but he knew she could hear. He wanted to look calm.

"Then why the hell yuh behaving like yuh is?" she shouted.

"So you want to tell the whole blasted world that that is not so? Why yuh don' jus make up your mind? Firs' you start your foolishness on the bus and then you coming with this . . ." He stopped. He realized that he was shouting too. "I don't know."

"I wasn' lying," she said quietly.

"I didn' say you were lying," Ferron said.

"You should be glad. You should be glad." She was raising her voice again. "I doing you a favor. Everybody got to know who Jesus is . . ."

"Oh shut up!"

"Ferron, don' tell me to shut up." She spoke slowly and quietly.

"I said yuh mus' shut up," he said again, this time not shouting.

They were silent for a few minutes. Then she spoke.

"Why yuh take everything so serious?" she asked softly.

"Because it is getting serious," he replied, staring ahead.

"But it musn', it musn'. You don' even know what

going happen nex' week; you don' know what I gwine do . . . I tell you things happening and—"

"Please, stop it, stop it. Forget it, alright, just forget it." He moved over to her. "Forget the whole blasted world."

"I don' know." She got up slowly. "I never did want this to happen."

"It's alright," he said. He did not believe himself.

"You don' know about me—"

"I don't want to know," he said.

They walked through the gate, and with the help of their flashlights they found the wooden cottage behind a small hillock in the middle of the grounds. They walked with arms around each other this time. It was dark and nobody could see them. They could not see themselves.

Unpublished notes of George Ferron Morgan

I was looking for the certificate and I found these letters. I wrote them in 1958. Cuba was freshly free. Revolution was so possible. It is hard for people to understand how possible it all seemed to us then— sometimes it even felt inevitable; we were just concerned about the spoils, how power would be divided. What a romantic warrior poet I was going to be. I believed in change. I really believed that there was a revolution coming to this island. Who was the man who wrote these words? I was not joking, I was serious. I was ready to slaughter the betrayers. Ready. I wrote to Locksley:

"I am worried that the watered-down socialist party might suddenly, in another election, pass from the scene, without the necessary preparation for a takeover. The boys who will be vital in this situation are not in the West Indies today; they are here in Notting Hill and Brixton. If we could throw 500 of those boys, who have become politically aware in this country, into the W.I. scene, the clowns in power now would disappear forever. They are the betrayers. And Locksley, with real working-class authority behind me, I should not have the slightest hesitation in shooting down these perpetually compromised politicians or any of the others, like my gracious and kind friend Rupert—he still preens about with the self-congratulatory look of pity and concern every time we sit to talk over a drink because he did me that favor; he lent me fifty pounds when I was at Oxford and starving, and even though I have paid him back, he continues to find ways to remind me of his kindness—well, he too will go down if he threatens to become offensive. It is a vital and fundamental issue *and there is no easy escape from it. If I myself waver, after fourteen years of conviction, when the crisis occurs, I give you full authority to shoot me down."*

TWENTY-TWO

The blackness was weightless, like a silk cloth around Ferron as he stood on the creaking porch. Above him the stars dusted the sky. From behind the two black hills, rising like round breasts in front of the cottage, there was a glow of amber light—the city. If he walked a few chains in either direction, moving away from behind the hills, he would see the city, like a jewel, glittering brightly behind the dark mounds. But the light was far away. Around him, the darkness was thicker, like an emptiness spreading deep into the surrounding trees. He could hear the faint rustle of leaves as breezes turned across the valley. The din of insects filled the night. He stared, trying to make his mind as empty as the dark space before him, trying to vomit out images that demanded thought, decisions—actual memories of the last month. He was trying to forget. It was difficult; things were closing in on him, his relationships were beginning to define themselves as mistakes, cumbersome, untidy mistakes with implications. People would get hurt, people would want to talk about feelings, about abandonment. His mind moved to Delores, still trying to make sense of the last weeks—was it the death or were the problems before that? Was it the rape, or was that too an excuse? And if it was the rape or the death, did that mean that the trauma would pass—that they could come back to a place of stability, of the consistency that they had known for a while? And would he always think about her, think about what she would feel in every situation he was in? He thought of Mitzie, Theresa—women with their own agendas, their own existences, who would suddenly stop the indulgence, the uncertainty of his actions, who would seek their own definitions, ways of understanding themselves and whatever he and they had together. He wanted this emptiness to last forever, but things were closing in on him, and he would have to see things ending soon. Soon, he knew, he would be alone—more alone than he had ever been before. It frightened him.

He could hear Mitzie moving around inside the cottage. She was washing the plates and pots that he had cooked with. He'd wanted to do it but she insisted. The domesticity of this shared activity bothered him; this is what had quickly taken over the cooking of the meal.

They were yet to settle on their sleeping arrangements. There was only one bed and it was barely large enough to hold both of them. He offered to sleep on the floor, somewhat embarrassed at finding only one bed—the other bed that was usually there had disappeared. It bothered him that she would think that he had planned it this way. He offered to sleep on the floor and she was amused.

"No man, me will sleep on the floor, 'cause I use to sleeping on floors, man." She grinned. "A man like you couldn' manage the floor, man."

He ignored her and made his bed on the floor. A thick blanket, a cotton sheet, another cotton sheet, and then a thicker blanket. He rolled up some clothes in a towel and patted it down as his pillow. She watched his ritual, then she patterned everything he did, making her bed on the floor beside him. They did this together in silence. When she was finished, they looked at each other and Ferron burst out laughing. It was a bit strained. Mitzie did not laugh. Ferron's laugh faded slowly to a nervous chuckle.

"You don' learn yet that yuh musn' spoil black people? 'Cause when you do that, them will climb all over yuh."

Ferron tried laughing again; he did not know what else to do. There was something about her tone that suggested that she was making a bigger point, but he was not sure. He was waiting for her to toss it back at him, his unease, his nervous laughter, his stupidity—the joke of it all. But she did not. Instead she started to hum a song. She unpacked some more of her things and the words became clearer: *"Sorry fe mawga dawg / Mawga dawg turn roun' bite yuh . . ."*

He walked to the kitchen to avoid another argument. There was something about Mitzie on this trip. A friend of his, a teacher from his sixth form days who had eventually become a friend, used to say all the time, "I know when they are ready to leave me; they start to pick fights. Sometimes they don't even know they are leaving." She was divorced three times by the time she was thirty. When they were eating Mitzie asked him if he spat in the food. He was tempted to get annoyed, but he thought of his friend's maxim and decided not to help her out. He said he hadn't. She said she had done that once, after seeing the film *The Color Purple*. She spat into the soup of a lady she was working for who was being a real bitch. She did it because she had a cold and she thought that it would mix well with the thick pea soup, and maybe it would afflict the woman with a dreadful cold. Eventually, the old lady did get a cold and that was like a curse on Mitzie because the woman was more miserable than ever.

"But it wasn't the same cold, you know, not like mine," she said. "'Cause the soup did well hot and it kill off them germs before them even come inside that woman. And anyway, that woman heart so bitter it would mash up any germs that mighta come near her. A real bitch. But it sweet me fe watch her eat that soup—an' me stand up right thereso in front of her, and it was like . . . It was like sex."

"Well, I never did it, but it wouldn't be a problem," he said. "After all, we know what our spit taste like, right—and you like how mine taste."

She stood up, leaned forward. As she moved he knew exactly what she was about to do. She let a thin line of spit drop into his plate. He stared at it, then looked at her. She was smiling. He mixed it into the rice and put a forkful into his mouth. He chewed it and swallowed it, staring at her.

"That is sick," she said.

"You think?" He continued eating. "I call it love."

She sat down and started to eat again. She kept looking at him, trying to probe his mind, as if asking a question, as they ate. The food was spicy and they were both sweating. They said nothing, but Ferron could feel things growing lighter, more sensual. He was sure of what was going to happen in the room that night.

He could hear her singing again, but he could not

recognize the song. She kept the tap flowing as she washed the dishes. He stared into the dark, trying not to think of the night to come, trying not to anticipate, to desire. Instead he thought of the next morning, them walking down the hill with a mess of confusion to re-solve. It would be over, he could tell, but the thought unsettled him.

She had wanted to be a singer. At first she was go-ing to be a gospel singer, but that was aborted after the business with her uncle. Now she wanted to sing good reggae and sweet rocksteady love songs. She had already been in the studio and had sung sweetly over a standard dub track (two chords, a rolling bassline). Ferron had heard it. Her voice was mellow, like an embrace. The mixture of the reggae and the distinctive sound of Mitzie, lazy, almost uninvolved, stirred something very sensual in Ferron. He wanted to hold her and dance when he heard the demo. She said she would be back in the stu-dio soon to do some backup for some popular singer, but she really wanted to do her own thing. Her friend, the sugar daddy, had promised to help her out. Ferron laughed at the idea.

"Hey, that man is a married man and him willing to help me better myself, alright?" She spoke with some ir-ritation. "You love go on like you better than everybody else, eh?"

"So what? You think he is using you?" Ferron asked.

"Him is helping me. I make my own decisions. Or you feel this whole business is a joke, right?" She stood and stopped the cassette, taking it out. "Some people like it, alright?"

"I like it. I wasn't saying that the—" He could see

that the damage had already been done. His attempts would sound condescending. "I was just worried about him taking advantage of . . ."

He heard nothing more about the music and her plans after that. It was hard to make it into Mitzie's world when she shut the door. He gave up.

As he thought of this, he could hear her voice coming closer behind him. The water was no longer flowing. Just her voice, soft in the night. Then she stopped singing.

"Sorry," she said quietly.

"For what?"

"I shouldn' spit in the food. That was a wicked piece a nastiness."

"No, no. I liked it. I mean, it was alright," he said. "But you alright?"

"Yeah man." She stayed behind him. "So you not vex with me?"

"No, I not vex."

"Yuh sure?"

"Yes," he said.

She moved beside him. She touched his face with her palm. It smelled of black pepper, onions, and lotion. He pulled her to him. She let her body gather around him. He spoke softly in her ears, a stream of words that came like the desire to cry for no good reason, like the aching of an orgasm at the verge. She held him and listened.

"I can remember being a baby. I know I can. Maybe it is those old pictures now turning yellow with age. It sounds like a poem, I know, but it is the only way to say it. A wild-eyed child with an unruly jungle of hair. I stared into the camera; I can remember doing that, staring into the camera; the camera was encased in brown leather, and the photographer wore brown trousers and a white shirt, and hard, dusty, black shoes. He wore black thick-rimmed glasses, but I can't remember his face. I knew to stare into the camera. But I can go further back. Back to when I was wrapped in the flesh and water of my mother where it was always warm, soft. My mother would lift me, kiss me with a sucking noise on my cheek with her lips wrapped over her teeth to protect me. She smelled of warm earth, sweet like a baby.

"I know what it tastes like—that milk in my mouth—light, thin. It came in a warm, seeping flow, filling my mouth before I realized it. I remember how to suck and swallow, pressing the breasts with my fist.

"It was a soft, half-lit world full of sensations—touching, touching. There is this feeling of weight inside my throat—it hurts . . . What have you done to me?"

She squeezed him tightly. He could feel the wet of her own tears on his chest. They held each other there in the cold.

His head fell down to her shoulders, his tongue touching the warmth of her skin. He nestled into the softness of her breasts, touching, cupping through the thin cotton. Moisture from his mouth soaked the fabric, but he could taste the sweetness of her milk seeping out.

"Don' taste it," she said.

"Uhuh." He kept licking.

"The milk coming down," she said. She held his head in place.

"Uhuh." Sucking through the fabric.

"Don't swallow it," Mitzie said from deep in her throat.

"Why?" he mumbled.

"Bad luck," she said, still holding his head against her.

"No," he said.

"Don't." Softer.

"Uhuh." He swallowed.

"Bad luck," she said.

"Sweet." His voice was slurred.

"You think you are a baby, nuh?" She rocked his head. There was playfulness in her voice.

"Uhuh." He swallowed again. His lips moved upward over her breasts, to her throat, to her mouth.

They kissed. Her tongue probed the inside of his cheek, prodded his teeth, pressed against his tongue.

"Well, if you feel yuh is a baby, yuh cyaan sleep on the floor, then. You have to sleep side a your mother," she said, walking inside the cottage. Ferron stood in the cold looking out. He heard Mitzie humming again. He walked inside to her.

She was beside him when he woke up. He had dreamed of the funeral, the undertaker, Mrs. Abrams, talking and talking, her hands pulling newspaper after old newspaper from a box and laying them before him. In his dream, the body had been buried; a long ceremony at a sunlit graveyard, and he had stood there crying, staring into the gaping grave. Mitzie was on the other side in black, looking at him. "Don't look down," she said. "Don't look down." Her face was hidden by a thick scarf, like the woman at the morgue, fanning imaginary flies from her face. Mitzie stood there looking at him.

There was a chill in the room. She was lying beside him with her face in his chest, her hands thrown around his body, sleeping deeply. They were on the floor. It was still dark. He began to talk. As he spoke, he could feel her stirring.

"I will remember everything 'bout this, everything. It can't leave me. You, this place, everything." He stopped. "I don't want to forget any of it. I don't want to understand any of it—"

"Me too," she said into his chest. "It did nice."

"I wish I knew he was in heaven," Ferron said.

"Maybe," she said, her mouth tickling his chest.

"You ever think of heaven, Mitzie? Of dying, and then going to somewhere?"

"That's where I going, yes. If anywhere at all, it mus' be there."

"You're sure." It was hard to tell if she was joking.

"I jus' know. God love me. I don' have nothing in me not to love," she said. "You know that. You know that."

"I know," he said, running his hand down her back. "I know."

"Yuh hungry?"

"Not really."

"Yuh stomach say yuh hungry," she said. "Yuh don' hear it?"

"It's because I don't know if I will see him there, you know," he said, still staring into the blackness. "Death is final, like when you dead Mitzie, tha's it—nothing else . . ."

"So life go, Ferron," she said softly.

"This thing won' last, will it?"

"It cyaan work. You an' me different. You don' want a woman like me. I have things to do and a man like you cyaan help me. I like you, Ferron, but me is not no dreamer. I want house and land, I want a good life, I want a life for my pickney—I want to sing, make a record." He tried to cut in, but she stopped him. "You, you want a mother right here now, Ferron. Not me. Tomorrow, you gwine look on this and say it was nice, and then. And then, tha's it. Nice." She was silent after that.

"One day, you will hear me on the radio, or read about me in a newspaper, and you will tell people how you know me and how they musn't be fooled. You will say: 'Cho, that guy? Go on like a real saint, eh? That one is a real hypocrite man; a real hypocrite.'" Ferron was not sure where that was coming from, but in a way he wanted to hurt her, wanted to show her that it hurt that she thought he was so inadequate, so unable to make her life meaningful. She was right, but it hurt that she said it like that—so casually, so confidently, so dismissively.

But she said nothing in reply to him. They lay there in silence for a while. Then he started to get up. She did not move.

"You really feel tha's how me stay?" she asked him.

"I don't know . . ."

"I woulda never say something like that, Ferron; never. I love you; you woulda never know how much yuh inna my skin, Ferron, you woulda never know." She buried her face in his neck. She started humming, the sensation of her throat vibrating against his body. He held her head, playing with her hair, massaging her skull slowly. He saw Mitzie in her blue jeans and white blouse walking away from him, gradually fading into a speck in his eye. He wondered whether they would meet in heaven.

Unpublished notes of George Ferron Morgan

They are all alive, all walking around in their own triumphant ways. They are comfortable. They are happy. Rupert, the hypocrite, has relished the opportunity to do me another favor by giving me this job when I had nothing else. So he continues to be painfully pitying—it is as if nothing has changed, and I am still that scholarship country boy from St. Ann, trying to be part of it all. And look at me. Well, there were no guns. There was no crisis. There was no fire burning down Kingston. We thought we had made the change, but we failed. Maybe it is my turn now to be gunned down. Me, the man in the middle, the man who can't seem to take a side, really. The man torn between the working class of my father and the middle class of my aspirations. Jesus. I need to get out of here . . .

TWENTY-THREE

Femi left the country a month later. They saw him off at the airport. Theresa cried a lot while they waved to him from the gallery. Afterward, they drove to Port Royal and she treated him to fish and festival. They walked along the black sand beach mostly in silence. He told her about Mitzie, about how he had been back to find her several days after they came off the hill. She had moved. It was difficult to believe that she had disappeared from his life so completely. It unnerved him, disturbed him. Theresa listened and reached to hold his hand. He let her hold his hand, as they continued to walk in silence.

Femi had done what he wanted to do. It was now properly in the psyche of the country that Old Man Ferron died under mysterious circumstances. Femi's book on the old man would be out in a year, and that would settle the issue once and for all. It all meant less and less to Ferron. The emptiness was far too complete.

His mother had written him asking why he did not go to see her. She said she felt the same emptiness, that even though the old man was no great husband, he was all she had, he was what she lived for. Now he was gone and there were the children, but they did not need her. She said she did not want to be a burden. Ferron read, saddened by his failure to be with her, to depend on her; saddened that he had to lie to her about Theresa. He had written her and told her of how much he missed the old man too.

Just under the shadow of the walls of Nelson's fortress, Theresa said she needed some distraction. She pulled Ferron to her and they began to kiss. Then she stopped, and asked how Delores was.

Delores was now in Miami. Delores had called to tell him she was going—she was migrating. She had said, "There is nothing for me in Jamaica." Her tone was brusque, a tone she put on when she'd worked every detail out and did not want anyone to try to change her mind. He'd asked what she would do in America. She was going to go to school, and then she was going to work with her father's brother who had a small business there that was growing. She did not plan to stay long in Miami. As soon as she had made enough money, she would move to somewhere like Oregon or North Dakota—somewhere as far from Jamaica and Jamaicans as she could manage. And she would be fine. Very fine, she said. He was tempted to make a joke about her proving to be a classic middle-class brown woman, but had thought better of it. She was not leaving for those reasons, not for social status, not for money. She was leaving, he knew, because she could not push from her mind the image of that man raping her. She was leaving because Ferron, her fiancé, had not protected her, was not willing to die for her; because the only person she'd expected to think of her as whole, after what had happened, could not bring himself to do so. She was leaving because she feared being raped again, and because everyone seemed to think she should get over it, that in Jamaica you just had to deal with that kind of thing.

He'd said, "Sorry, Delores."

"For what?" she'd asked. There was a hint of tenderness in her voice, which made him continue.

"For everything—for hurting you, for not being able to help you, for abandoning . . ."

"It's okay," she said. "It's okay. Shit happens." She'd asked him about his woman. He told her that Mitzie had disappeared. She said, "Poor Ferron, everybody leaving you. Eh?"

For days he kept changing his mind about whether she was being sarcastic or sincere. In the end he realized it was both. He asked if she wanted him to come to airport.

She said, "If you have to ask . . ." and left it at that.

He did not go to the airport. Another of his failings.

He did not tell Theresa all this. He just said that Delores had left the island and things were done with them. Theresa said, "Hush, baby," and this was pure pity, which made him uncomfortable, because it was clear that she saw him as a victim of failed affection, like her. Two pathetic people losing the ones they cared about. He could not explain that what Femi was doing to her was nothing like his mess, but that would have been pointless. She squeezed his hand in solidarity and pulled him along.

They got back to his apartment at midnight. She asked if she could pick him up in the morning to go to the country. She explained that she wanted nothing meaningful from their relationship, just the company. She had taken a few days off work to recover from Femi's departure. He said he would be waiting. But as he spoke he knew he would already have left town to go up to the old family house in St. Ann before she arrived next morning. He would be somewhere else, trying to find something that he still did not know quite how to define.

It was still dark when he walked across the dew-sodden lawn to the bus stop. Theresa would cry, but she would be alright.

Unpublished notes of George Ferron Morgan

For the time being, I suppose I should stay here. The money is horrible, but anything is better than walking home with nothing. I get to carry my briefcase. I leave in the mornings as if off on a mission—off to work. The neighbors see me in my bush jacket leaving early, and see me return in the evenings. There is dignity in this. When they run into me, I can say, "I am at the Gleaner," so it seems as if I am alive, as if I am bouncing back, as if nothing has happened. But a lot has happened. It is a lie. I have nothing. I have no money. I am depending on my wife to look after us, to pay the rent, to hold it together. I am waiting every day for word from somewhere saying that I can be useful, I can have some dignity. I wish I had the gumption to do myself in. I wouldn't know where to start, really. But this is what a suicidal man's life looks like. Not hopeless. It is never hopeless in and of itself. It is just the fall. The distance of the fall that declares the hopelessness. I can't stay here, though. It is killing everything in me. The absurdity of what we are doing. The idiocy of trying to pretend. The letter came from the high school in Mandeville. They want me there. So I will go. At least there I will be useful, will relish what I am doing. There I can construct new fictions for myself. There I will not have to face the dark house every evening, the despair of counting pennies, the weight of my uselessness, their eyes staring at me with pity.

Sometimes I think it is better to avoid certain thoughts. I have been avoiding love. I can't write about love here. I am so intent on my vitriol that to speak of love would break me. This morning I wept in the cab coming in. Much of this seems pathetic, and I fear I will start weeping as I write this. One of those women will notice, and the whispering will start. But I will take that job, so why should I care now? Perhaps I should weep. Perhaps I should create an episode of scandalous insanity. Like that poet—such a good poet—who took to walking through the lanes of uptown stark naked for a week. He never made the papers. His family, you see, and there is that power here still—the power of family and connections. But his was such a grand gesture. I should attempt it. But all I am doing is distracting myself from speaking of love. I wept because I looked back this morning, to see my wife standing there watching me drive out. I watched her turn to the hibiscus hedge and finger one of the flowers. That simple gesture of tenderness broke me. No matter what I do now, I can only feel gratitude to her. I have left her with nothing. I have taken her from her rooting, from those people who could care for her and lift her up, and brought her to this. Now she sits there in front of me, while I crack the shell of a soft-boiled egg, and she tells me with gentle pragmatism that they are wicked, all of them, all the hypocrites who have called me their friends, and she tells me that I should go and teach in that high school, and she reminds me that I started teaching in high school and I loved it, and she reminds me that I am a brilliant teacher, and she reminds me that she has taken so much from me, the drinking, the smashed cars, the fights, the women, and she has still loved me. And there she is, standing by the hedge, fingering the petals of the hibiscus. For the last year, she has moved around like a woman in mourning. I did not realize this at once. In fact, I only realized it a few months ago. She has been mourning me. She speaks to me as if I am already dead. It is with awe, but with a curious sense of resignation—a sense that nothing really has to change. And when she is not watching me, I see the way she moves, the slow deliberate walk, the self-sufficiency in her handling of matters, the respect shown to me, never arguing, but a kind of adoration, even, and I know that she is mourning me—that I am dead. I wish I could say that it makes me sad, or makes me feel awful. It doesn't. In some strange way, it makes me feel deeply loved. Of course, this makes sense. She does love me. She has loved me despite my waywardness. But this morning, I was covered with such sorrow about that. About how pathetic we now are. She is watching her husband pretend to be employed, leaving in a taxi we can barely pay for, going off to make money that makes not even a dent in the debts we have; going off before she puts herself together to start to conduct the miracles of the day to keep us alive. I love her. She was always beautiful, that face, those sharp cheeks, that brilliant smile, those hips, those glorious hips, that blackness in her, that ennobling blackness in her.

None of this will stay. It is sentimental. It counts for nothing, really. Two hours trying to make this something useful. I am hungry. My last meal. I should strip to my drawers and stand on my desk and howl.

This morning I saw that white Toyota again. It swung behind the cab on Barbican Drive and stayed with us all the way down Lady Musgrave Road, down Hope Road, past Cross Roads, and then tucked into one of the law offices just up the road. I stepped out of the cab and looked directly at two of the men who were leaning on the car smoking, shades masking their eyes. I have imagined them as the bearers of my death. But that seems so pointless. Sometimes I think that Vera Chen has actually set them on me to protect me. Well, they will have no one to follow next week.

This country suddenly feels so small. So damned small and petty.

TWENTY-FOUR

I t is a hot day. The sky is simply blue. Stretching. The sea beats the pebbled beach. Wind. Against the green of the hillside, the black road twists in the shape of the coast. The minivan called chariot hurtles breakneck, avoiding death, although there is death everywhere, like the rapid-fire DJ resists the collapse of words into nonsense—just sounds tumbling—by deft acrobatics of the tongue. In white flowing robes, the conductor swings with the wind from the doorway of the van, laughing.

Conductor: We going now.
Ferron: How far is it from here?
Conductor: We are going, we are going . . .
Ferron: How far, to . . . ?
Conductor: On this red, gold, green train . . .
Ferron: To Sturge Town . . . ?
Conductor: On this red-a, gold . . . en-a green train . . .
Ferron: Excuse me, sir . . .
Conductor: Tickets . . . Tickets . . .
Ferron: Excuse me, sir . . .
Conductor: Sturge Town to Kingston . . . Not far . . .

Burning Spear eats up the asphalt. The van finds its rhythm in the bass and drum, and settles on the road, low, steady, the tires soft and sticky. Handling well, the turnings are easy.

Fern Gully is a snake's head. It starts on the Devil's Mountain and spews its store of sperm into the sea where the eight rivers meet. There is a prostitute there who Ferron remembers. She was twelve and he was thirteen and she frightened him with her bold eyes and her sharp bony hips. They ran and ran along the beach. He paid her five dollars, and when she was finished she straightened her black lace dress and leaned against a coconut tree trunk changing her shoes. That was yesterday, and the old man was dead and sailing to become ashes in a rented hearse. A black taxicab.

Ferron: Yes . . . Yes . . .
Conductor: Small up yourself, daughter . . . Press, driver . . .

Through the car window, the smell of pimento. The old man is awake, his eyes are bright, trying to see around the corners of the hill, not able to wait for the next magical vision. The old man is so much younger, drumming out a rhythm on the steering wheel nervously.

I have, says Ferron from under a cloud, I have walked the paths you roamed, have smelled the spice of pimento, have clasped the old hands, in your colored world, kept cool in the mountain air, and the overgrown paths. We met on the road in the bush where Femi levitated, talking to you.

The old man smiles.

What did you say? Ferron asks him slowly. What did you say to Femi, in the bushes there? You said something. You were speaking about me. My head was swelling.

The car strains up the hill. Changing gears, changing gears. The old man is drumming a rhythm on the sweat-slick steering wheel. His beard is streaked with gray. There is cotton in his nose. Ferron reaches across and pulls out the cotton. There is dry blood on the cotton. Ferron throws the cotton from the window. It floats up into clouds.

There is a path, the old man says, as the crow flies, from the house on the hill to the school. It comes out there. Used to walk that path every day, while your grandfather walked the road in his black suit and straw hat. I think sometimes he thought he was back in Warri greeting the natives with a bow. I would try and get to the school before him. There, there is Breadfruit Bend, because of the trees. There used to be more. Donkey Grove over there, Star-Apple Corner because so many city people would drive off the corner, Tamarind Arch . . .

The old man is proud of the recollections, giving each sharp bend in the road the endearment of such names. His laughter is nervous nearing the house, the child in him drumming out the tattoo.

Old man: And flying over France, I would imagine from up there what this old cracked house would look like from above. The rusting zinc, the pimento barbecues, the groves and groves of bush. Then the plane would be suddenly lighter. Tiny explosions of light and smoke far below us. From the sky, this house would look like paradise. It was like bombing your own home. And he is always talking.

Ferron: You said something to him . . .

Old man: We are doing this for history. Context. Your
grandparents are buried here . . .

Ferron: Did you want to be buried here?

Old man: I thought about it a lot. When I was a young
man in London, I did . . . Now . . .

Ferron: I don't know what we did with the ashes. I left
them at the funeral home, I think . . . Maybe they
have them still...

Old man: Coping mechanism?

When he smiles his small brittle teeth glint yellow in the sun.

Ferron: How did you really die?

Old man: The blood exploded in my brain, you saw it . . .

Ferron: They pushed you. They did, didn't they? That is
what this is about.

Old man: Lucas said they pushed me from the top of the
stairs.

The old man is laughing at himself.

Old man: I think I felt something. Pushing, and I fell
through as if flying.

*The trees encroach on the house. It has become green, the
planks of wood for walls are gray-green in the shade. The
awnings are peeling. Metal awnings as rusted as the zinc
roof. The windows open wide, crucifixes in boxes. The goats
graze nonchalantly. There is no one around.*

Old man: That is the house. That is the house there, broken and sun-beaten. It used to be green. Come . . .

Ferron: We can't, the fence is too high . . .

Old man: Hold my hand. We will fly . . . fly . . .

Ferron: Jesus . . . we are flying . . . How?

> *Now on the porch, the two stand and stare at the line at the edge of the sea, where it spills over into nothing. On a clear day, you can see Cuba. On a clear simple blue-sky day.*

Old man: I used to play on this porch. Scratched out worlds in my tiny head. Look there. Do you see it?

Ferron: What?

Old man: Cuba. Cuba. When Wayne left, and Nettie and Fiona, it was me and the two old ones. They told me about Africa, and then one day he showed me Cuba. It was early, early, pink in the sky, and Cuba was there, green in the haze. It had always been there, I just did not know . . . I told this to Fidel, this story. He touched my forehead with his lips and called me comrade. His hip pocket bulged. He never pulled out his gun. He said it was too heavy. He only pulled it out to use it.

> *Augustus and Laura are identical twins with the same gray-green eyes and short white hair, wispy in the wind. Their skin is cocoa-pod yellow, and they tremble their thin hands when they speak. Augustus finishes every sentence Laura speaks in his head. He has heard everything she has said this week and it is only Monday. They wince at the sunlight, watching this man try to play a game of cricket without bat and ball on the overgrown front lawn. The son is playing too.*

Augustus: What you want here, sah? I can help you? Who
   you is?

Ferron: Sorry, I . . .

Laura: Is who out there, Augustus? The man on the
   porch, is who?

*In the light you can see the distracted stare of Laura. She
sees things in thick woolly shapes now. There is light green,
orange, yellow, but all in thick woolly shapes. She discovers
pictures by the pattern of words.*

Augustus: Is alright, woman, calm yourself. Yes, boss . . .

Ferron: I . . . my father used to live here, years ago. We
   own the place . . . My family, I . . .

Augustus: Is Teacher Morgan people, Laura . . . Is the
   fornicating gran'son. Sexual sins missis, sexual. Jees
   U, I shoulda guess. Look on the nose . . . What I can
   do for you, sah? We stop sen' the rent after we never
   get back no receipt, an' it look like the people them
   dead off. You aunty . . . Which part you park the car?
   We never hear it at all . . .

Ferron: I didn't drive. Walked up the hill . . . I mean we
   flew.

Augustus: Oh. I see . . . Easier. Well, about the rent . . .

Ferron: No, not the rent. I just came to see the place. My
   father is dead, and I came to talk to him.

Laura: Augustus. Who? Lawd, what a way the man favor
   Teacher Morgan. Voice strapping same way . . . An'
   correc'. Very correc'.

Ferron: You knew them . . .

Laura: Everybody roun' here know them, son. Dem teach
   mos' everybody—

Augustus: Him never come 'bout rent, Laura. Find the man a drinks, eh . . . or a mango. 'Im jus' come to talk to the old man. You know that man could teach you anything. Listen to this. Wait, wait. First, tell me how old you think I is . . . Tell me.

He looks like a man a hundred and fifty years old, not because he looks frail because he is not frail—his body is erect, his limbs tightly muscled, his face handsome in the purest ways that man can be handsome. But his eyes have the depth of time, as if he has lived forever.

Ferron: Seventy-five . . .

Augustus: Ha ha. Laura, Laura, you hear that? Bwai, put on twenty years to that, quick-quick. Alright, so hear me now. Listen me. I learn this when I was six years old.

He opens up his chest, raises his hand, and begins. Laura watches with a mixture of pride, indulgence, and slight impatience with a show-off.

Augustus:
I see you stand like greyhounds in the slips,
Straining upon the start. The game's afoot:
Follow your spirit, and upon this charge
Cry "God for Harry, England, and Saint George!"

Laura: Dyam colonizers!

Augustus's eyes are wet.

Augustus: Your grandfather teach me that, and I teach your old man. I teach him all kinda things.

Laura: Ah, that one. Won't stop drive up an' down, up
   an' down. Singing all kinda song. A fornicator too?
Ferron: I don't think so. I don't know. No one lives an
   exemplary life.
Augustus: Maybe not. But why not? Man is man.
Laura: Man is man, fi true.

*Augustus almost speaks those words for her because she
takes so long to say them. They are smiling.*

*The old man is laughing. Sometimes they cannot see him,
but they have heard him marching up and down with his
cane as a rifle to the shoulder.*

> We peasants, artisans, and others,
> Enrolled among the sons of toil,
> Let's claim the earth henceforth for brothers,
> Drive the indolent from the soil
> On our flesh too long has fed the raven
> We've too long been the vulture's prey,
> But now farewell the spirit craven
> The dawn brings in a brighter day

*He has forgotten the words already . . . He chuckles. Fer-
ron looks at him. Ferron remembers the words like a buried memory, like another language with sounds he knows,
meanings he knows, but with words he cannot recognize.
He sings.*

Ferron:
   Then comrades, come rally,
   And the last fight let us face,

The internationale unites the human race,
Then comrades, come rally,
And the last fight let us face,
The internationale unites the human race.

Old man: It did not die in me with Gorbachev and Yeltsin. I prefer Mamba socialism. There somebody keeps hearing you screaming, "I told you we could do it, Yankeee!"

Ferron: Where are they buried? My grandparents. They are buried here, somewhere . . .

Augustus: Only the teacher. The wife buried at Dovecot in town. Teacher buried in the back, with him father and mother . . . And the pigeons been laying eggs in the rafters ever since. Nobody don't want to touch the old hut. That thing must be over one hundred years now. Bush and piece a old cedar. But the pigeon dem like it . . .

Ferron: Show me . . .

Augustus: Right by the lickle patch of tree. Nobody don't go there again so the bush grow over, you know? Over beyond thereso. That is the path. Not many people walk that way these days . . .

The path here is thick. Down into a small valley where the earth is soft and wet and thick weeds grow and twist about the waist. Then there is the slope which you climb till your face is pimpled with sweat, and you look back and stare at the house glowing against the sea's green and blue. Beyond the coffee bushes is a dark cave of green where, in a mound of cement, lies the past.

Ferron: Thank you.

It is still now.

Old man: They said their ghosts hover above the house,
   my grand ones, swooping down, one wind lifting a
   tattered sheet's edge—animation, now brilliant O,
   shifting breadfruit leaves to a rustle and watching
   eyes glow toward the hills.
Ferron: Did you go to heaven?
Old man: Have you screwed Mitzie yet?
Ferron: There are reasons for everything.
Old man: Slumming with the lumpen, eh?
Ferron: I am mourning your death. We do strange things
   when we mourn.

   Ferron feels he is betraying something. The old man is no
   longer standing there. The voice is nothing all of a sudden.
   Ferron looks for Mitzie. She is leaning on a post in a black
   lace dress. She is smiling. Her body is moving slowly until,
   like a pneumatic drill, it begins to batter the earth. He has
   no money in his pocket. She asks for love instead. He tries
   to find it.

Old man: You want to know where they went.
Ferron: To heaven?
Old man: I always wondered about that. I was worried I
   would never see them . . . I plan to be in heaven . . . I
   used to talk to them when I was a boy. Friends, you
   know. They seemed to crawl from the roots of the
   trees and stand there in white, smiling. They always
   had a message for me. They have a message for you,
   now. They are carrying the kola nut in their fists,

waiting with a knife to share it . . . I played around the gray tombs . . .

Augustus and Laura watch the two playing cricket and ramping in the bushes. Ferron starts to run through the trees, trying to remember where the paths are. The old man, feeling lazy, does not follow. Ferron is trying frantically to remember. Laura and Augustus look on.

Laura: Him looking very strange. Where him going?
Augustus: By the graveside. The man looking for roots . . .
    Even fornicators have roots.
Laura: Sexual . . .
Augustus: What?
Laura: Sexual . . .
Augustus: Yes.

Augustus thinks that perhaps Laura has not heard the word from her brain properly. She is supposed to say, "Wish him all the best." But the way that word has made her smile makes him think better of correcting her. Sometimes she has her own mind and it takes her to places he has never been to. He lets her go. She always comes back, smiling.

Laura: You hearing what I hearing?
Augustus: Going mad. Is like Teacher Morgan duppy a
    ride him . . . The spitting image . . .
Laura: Call Rastaman Lewis. Mek him bring the drum . . .

Ferron's heart feels as if it will give way on him. The blood is rushing too quickly.

Ferron: These overgrown paths where, fired with Arthurian legends, you galloped, mad-child on a wild irreverent steed, dizzy in the patchwork of sunlight through branches.

The child overwhelms the adult, and now Ferron is sprinting, beating hoofbeats against his chest, light blazing green on his face; grass and bramble rushing at him and cutting across his body, whipping him. He keeps running like that, in and out of light, under the cry of the dizzy hawk spiraling in the simple blue sky. His shouts echo in the tree trunks.

The Rastaman beats the drums and sings. Ferron is stopped by the sound. He looks around. The light is fading very quickly. It will soon be morning.

Old man: They think you are oppressed by a spirit.

Ferron: I have wanted to talk to you. That is why I came here. I hoped you would be here . . .

Old man: They will continue to play the drums until you calm down . . .

Ferron: I never did speak to you about them. About her. Your mother. She thought we were a nuisance . . .

Old man: You were too young. Too young when she died . . .

Ferron: But she came back here. At the funeral, I thought of her flying across the island all night until she reached Sturge Town and this graveside.

Old man: She must have traveled all night . . .

Ferron: And then you came to her, when you had traveled, and she was waiting . . .

Old man: I praise the glorious summers of pimento . . .

Ferron: I should see her . . .

Old man: Over there, on the barbecue. She has been waiting a long time for this—for you to come back . . .

*On the barbecue where dry brown pimento beans roast, the
ancient chair she sits in is there where a rotting orange tree
leans and sheds acrid leaves. The chair is light and fading,
sucked dry by sun and salt wind. See her bandannaed there,
sharp calico against the hill's gray; earth mother, her wrinkled hands outstretched, trembling; her eyes glowing. She
looks nothing like the photograph. Here, her eyes are open.
Ferron touches, trying to find his way back.*

Old man: She is smiling. She is happy to see you . . .
Laura: Slow him down now. Him coming down now.

*A shot cuts across the evening. Birds, in massive flocks of
black spots against the sky, rush from the bushes and call
into the night. Then there is silence. On the barbecue there
is blood. Sheets and sheets of material, simple cotton
sheets, dance animated on the barbecue, trying to cover
the bloodstains.*

Conductor: Browns Town. Sturge Town, St. Ann's Bay!
Ready one, Ready . . . one. Your time, driver . . .

*Praise the silent homecoming, praise the songs of the ghosts
sealed in my mind's chrysalis, praise the constant leaves
spinning in the pure air, praise the hands that birthed,
worn as they are, for they glow, stained red with first blood,
spilled into the navel-string soil where for years the ancient
red-barked trees have stood. Praise these things.*

Old man: I can't tell you a damned thing about this space. Can't tell you a thing about this crazy house on the hill. Don't fall back. I may not be behind you. What did I say to Femi? Trump card. I keep that hidden; you will keep asking of me. Dead people have pride too. It's all like magic.

He says this with that twinkling eye and that laugh. As if the death, the whole morbid incident, was a grand scheme for attention.

Old man: I like Mitzie, though. Well, Delores gone to Miami. Everybody have their reasons. Five years ago is pure capitalist run to Miami, now is pure lapse socialist gone to Miami. Same story, running and running and running away, but you cyaan run away from yourself . . . Anyway, her hips was just too low for the baby business, nuh so you say? You can bawl now, Ferron. You mess her up good. But it will pass too, like everything else.

There is big laughter. Femi, Kamau, and Quackoo, and now the old man, emptying their stomachs of everything. Ferron is watching from the darkness, still waiting.

It is morning.

Burning Spear's hypnotic bassline thumped in the back of his head. The green sunlight, filtered through the clutter of leaves around his window, woke him. He stood on the porch and looked out to the village that spread beneath him, and then to the island, and then the sea, a flat glassy surface stretching to the line of the sky's beginning. Somewhere to his right, on a clear hill, stood the white chapel with its crucifix piercing the blue sky. The bell sounded, calling the believers to service.

Alone on the hill, Ferron could feel the gathering of everything he thought he understood about living and dying, and as he studied these things, he found that he had nothing to speak of. So he slept through the ritual of days, riding the enchantment of a reggae man, playing the steady predictability of sound with uncanny success—every sound was a way to move, to breathe, to walk. For Ferron, this was the stability he wanted to understand. Something simple, something void of the complexities of meaning. He watched the island from the porch as morning turned hot and relentless in the sky.

AFTERWORD

Driving along the smooth belly of the coastal roads, the voices of Caribbean poets danced through the car, intoning a landscape and a way with words that seemed so ancient, that seemed to be of another time, and yet so ageless and true. He thought of the poems and books he had written—this he who is an I, but who must create a he to allow the fiction to generate its own chaos of meaning. And these poems, these poems carried with them the complex laboring of poets who tried to make words soar, soar into the heavens. It was a bad recording, cracking, muffled, but the words of the dead came back to him, came back with nostalgia and this story of a history and a place. These were the voices of those who had come to pay tribute to a dead writer, and now, fifteen years later, so many of them were dead:

. . . We are burying our brains,
our Rhodes Scholars, our people of letters,
and the tenured, nailed-down intellectuals;

but we fear the village is emptying
quickly, and the children, untethered, have
abandoned the kraal. They leave the frames

of the houses to sway in the dust,

and the words that remain in the trees
grow jaundiced with overuse.

The way the words transport him from this long
black road lined by groves of high-smelling wisteria,
and the dense green of swamp bush, where among the
clutter of trees, warm, ticking, police patrol cars lie in
wait for some dreaming soul, feet too heavy on the pedal,
trying to fly when flying is the only logical thing to do—
the way the words carry him to another place is the way
stories begin.

At home, still unsteady from the dream of the ride,
still trying to piece together a true history of the time
so long ago that myths have taken root and it is hard
to tell the truth from the story that has made the truth
palatable—the story that seems so much better—he is
startled by the recollection of things that were hidden
away, by the presence of voices he had forgotten were
there in that theater giving tribute to the dead writer.
In this place of remembering there is a spark of a story
taking shape. And with the children gathered around,
he sticks the cassette into the tape deck and lets it run.

On a tape, never before heard, is a muffled recording, a BBC recording of over thirty years ago, a time after
Fidel was triumphant and Nkrumah had declared the
dream of a United States of Africa, a time when he was a
seed taking shape in his mother's belly, this voice comes
back over time, and the children stop somersaulting and
shout: "That's Daddy, that's Daddy!" And indeed, the
voice, with all the inflections, all the smooth and slight
tenor of its tone, is his voice; it could be no one else but
his voice. He embraces the children and tells them that

it is their grandfather. They do not understand. He does not try to explain, for he, too, startled by the familiar in the voice, plays it back again and again. There are no discernible words, just this wash of a voice carrying over time.

From this far, all memory must take shape in fiction. From this far, even the sacred becomes the fodder for myth. From this far, the voice repeated becomes a ritual of making things again and again. There is a great fiction in this story that is told that must be so. From a backward glance comes a way of placing the contradictions of our life into perspective, only to shatter them again. But this is the way of the world.

In the house next door, a woman stands mute and dumb; the gallons of whiskey cannot blunt the pain. A man lies passed out on the sofa in a suit. Two girls lie in bed weeping. Their brother, who was in age between them, walked into a truck and died. Everything he was is gone, and the house next door is dead; the simple wreath tells us to tremble as we pass. The woman steps out with a cigarette in her mouth, her eyes are red, her hair is disheveled. The child was not her own, but the child was the child of her lover, the child was her child. He hated her, but he came into her arms and wept when he felt pain. Now she stands mute, staring into the vacant parking lot. This death sweeps the apartment complex, and nothing moves, nothing moves.

He has lived to make words unfold like this, lived to leave a legacy of errors, of lies, of myths, of dreams. The ending of the book is inevitable in this world of the dead. In many ways, this story comes back because of remembrance, but in others, it comes back because of fear of what might have been.

The tape keeps playing over and over into the small hours of the night. His wife calls him up to check one of the children. He wakes in another place. Then he falls asleep again, staring at the green light of the tape deck, rising and falling, tracing the cadence of his voice, a clue, a gene track going so far back, so far back.

KWAME DAWES's debut novel *She's Gone* (Akashic) was the winner of the Hurston/Wright Legacy Award (Debut Fiction). He is the author of twenty-one books of poetry and numerous other books of fiction, criticism, and essays. In 2016, his book *Speak from Here to There*, a cowritten collection of verse with Australian poet John Kinsella, was released along with *When the Rewards Can Be So Great: Essays on Writing and the Writing Life*, which Dawes edited. His most recent collection, *City of Bones: A Testament*, was published in 2017. His awards include the Forward Poetry Prize, the Hollis Summers Poetry Prize, the Musgrave Silver Medal, several Pushcart Prizes, the Barnes & Nobles Writers for Writers Award, and an Emmy Award. He is Glenna Luschei Editor of *Prairie Schooner* and is Chancellor Professor of English at the University of Nebraska. Dawes serves as the associate poetry editor for Peepal Tree Press and is director of the African Poetry Book Fund. He is series editor of the African Poetry Book Series—the latest of which is *New-Generation African Poets: A Chapbook Box Set (Sita)*—and artistic director of the Calabash International Literary Festival. Dawes is a Fellow of the Royal Society of Literature, and in 2018 was elected as a Chancellor of the Academy of American Poets.